Honey Jane, Sexpot Extraordinaire

Disclaimer:

This book contains depictions of endowed women. While the characters are hermaphrodites, this is not in any way intended as a depiction- serious or fetishized- of intersex individuals. That is a real condition that affects real people.

It is a light-hearted erotica in which women are fucked by other women- with dicks. They are a fictional subset of humanity in a slightly dystopian setting, where humanity faces extinction from infertility, both male and female.

Please note, this story also contains themes of pregnancy, fertility and infertility caused by early onset menopause. All depictions are for story purposes and are not intended to be wholly scientifically accurate. Once again, this story is set in a fictional parallel universe.

Please do not take this story as true representations of either. Research has been done into the hermaphrodism of other biological organisms, as well as the symptoms and effects of early menopause, but this is for fictional realism only.

Thank you for reading.
Please enjoy.

Meet The Characters

Honey Rose

29 years old

School teacher

Alicia Padrilla

24 years old

Gym instructor

Ariana Padrilla

32 years old

Senior Researcher

Enrique Padrilla

35 years old

Data Marketing

Emilia Lottery

35 years old

Model

Lily Lottery

5 years old

Dr Rani
Kudira

Jessica

22 years old

Nanny

Marcella Robbins

30 years old

Gym owner and instructor

Alicia

She was at the gate again.

I adjusted my shades as I tilted my head, just enough to convince anyone watching that I was impatiently waiting for the kids to be released, when in fact, my eyes were resting very patiently on a certain kindergarten teacher's round mounds. What a fine specimen they were. A creamy weighted pair that threatened to spill right out of her satin blouse as she turned to face the emerging line of students, granting me a delicious glimpse of her derriere.

She bent to ~~fix~~ grab a fallen lunchbox off ~~of~~ the ~~bag table~~ floor, and I fought to remain composed as I felt a slight twitch in my sweatpants. There was a beautiful new position to add to my ever-growing collection of fantasies at night.

Not that I hadn't already considered the thought of her spread on all fours like my own personal pet…indeed, that was my favourite one, since the first day I met her during the children's Christmas assembly, in *just that pose*. Five years in the small town of Windermere, Florida, and I'd never seen her. Or if I did, certainly not like *this*. She was reaching for a runaway bauble under the desk, completely oblivious to the fact that she was seconds away from being impaled right where she lay, ass up, head down, the green knitted cables of her skirt pulling taught against her hips.

Just the memory of our first encounter, and the humping that ensued, sent another frission up my spine, and I felt myself twitch more violently. I coughed and took a step back, subtly adjusting myself, ensuring there was no sign of my excitement.

Pervy, I know, but I felt quite confident in the fact that no one present knew of my slow-mounting obsession. Afterall, who would expect such lecherous thoughts from dearest Lily Lottery's favourite aunt?

Honey

Thank goodness it's almost Friday, I thought to myself as I ushered the kids out of their hazardously spread line and into their parents' arms.

 A chorus of "Bye Miss Janey!" echoed around me as I struggled to keep up with each departing child, ~~crouching to keep up with each~~ as they dropped bags, coats and bottles alike. Only once the initial stream had passed did I straighten and make my way back towards the last few five-year olds waiting by the classroom door.

 Among them was one of my favourite students, little Lily Lottery, an adorable child with a name just as sweet.

As I made my way from the class gate to the door, I was reminded of why I was so attached to her- she reminded me of myself. Slight and shy, with dark locks framing her round face, although her waves were slightly more tamed than my own aptly named honey curls, especially in the heat of the budding summer. My cheeks were fuller than the young child's, her green eyes were much more vibrant than my dull blue, making me feel slightly pathetic for even comparing. Those green orbs peered up at me now.

"Can you see your parent, Lily?" I asked her, reaching out a hand as I waved off the last two children to their parents. Lily's hand clasped mine as we made our way to the gate.

"I can see my *tita* Alicia," she whispered, and I turned to follow her little fingers, waving towards a tall, muscled figure by the trees. As the figure waved back and advanced towards us, her silhouette became clearer. As it did so, revealing her features to me fully, I bit back a gasp.

Since the start of the year, I heard much about Lily's family, particularly during the 'Family Tree' projects of the autumn term. I knew she had parents who worked long hours, a nanny who was less than attentive, and a string of older cousins on her mother's side who tormented her.

 Her mother's side of the tree had filled the page, whereas her father's side only had three branches- his and his two sisters, Alicia and Ariana. All I knew of them was that they were of Latin American descent, with Lily taking her mother's last name, and that all three

Padrilla siblings were estranged from their adoptive parents now, hence the blank spaces on the sheet. Having met Mr Lottery, average man of average build with a head of sandy blond hair, I had always assumed Lily's dark coloring came from her mother's Italian side. But as I watched the gorgeous Latina woman walk towards me, I was startled by just how familiar she seemed.

She towered over my 5'5 frame, and even through the loose jacket she had on, I noticed the thick curl of muscled shoulders, suggesting she was not unacquainted with the small town's only gym. She wore thick sweatpants in the middle of the April heat, and I couldn't help but flush when I realised they curved over a toned ass that flexed smoothly as she bent down and lifted her niece into her arms, with barely a sweat.

"Hola Lilypad," she said, coaxing giggles out of the usually shy child. I couldn't help but smile as I watched the young child laugh, wishing I could have my own. But at 29, with no sign of a boyfriend in sight, and a near endless stream of early onset menopause reminders slipping through my mailbox, I doubted I'd get a chance before the doctor's inevitably tell me I'm too old to try naturally. The birthrate had declined significantly across the last decades, with more and more women falling into menopause before their 30th birthday, resulting in a boom in adoption, fertility clinics and a sharp decline in sperm count across men globally. For larger cities, it didn't seem to cause much of a stir till recently, but for small town girls like me in Windermere? It meant even if you found a man, he probably couldn't give you a child anyway.

I tried not to focus on that somber thought as I watched this Amazon goddess brush her hair aside, revealing startling green eyes, same shade but different shape as Lily's, a sharp nose, and even sharper jaw below full rose lips. Not for the first time, I wondered about my sexuality as I found myself utterly entranced by the woman before me.

There *is a woman who could get any man she wanted.*

Or woman.

"Hola, Miss Janey." Her voice was smooth, rich and melodious, and for a moment, I forgot what the appropriate response was, too caught up in the way her tongue wrapped around the vowels.

"Hi! You must be Alicia- I'm Janey. Well." I blushed a bit harder, cursing my pale skin as Alicia's grin slowly grew wider. "I'm Honey, Honey Jane, but the kid's call me Janey."

"I know, we've met before-"

My mind blanked a bit as I tried to recall ever meeting Lily's aunt. Surely, I would have remembered?

"-Of course, it wasn't face to *face.*"

My heart stopped for a moment as it hit me- Last year's Christmas show! I had gotten stuck searching for a bauble under the desk, where it had fallen off of the class tree (resulting in a lot of tears and placating marshmallows until showtime, during which I slipped away to find the treasured item), when a kind parent – or so I thought- helped pull me out, after a lot of pulling and shoving. By the time I'd cleared my hair from my face, the classroom was empty, and I was swept up into the mess of organizing Christmas for five-year-olds.

My eyes glanced back down to her arms, the muscles deliciously on display as the hoodie had slipped ~~down~~ open with Lily's movements, also revealing a defined chest in a tank top. *I didn't even know you could muscle your breasts!*

"Yes, I forgot about that, thank you for your help. I was quite stuck!" It *can't* have been possible to flush any harder.

She smirked. *"It was my pleasure."*

And yet, flush harder I did.

Alicia

I drove Lily home, enthusiastically singing along with her to every rainbow pop song that came up on the radio.

As the bland singer encouraged listeners to '*shake it off*', I found myself contemplating how lovely Honey Jane's ass proceeded to do just that as she ran back to the safety of her classroom, flushed red all the way down to her chest. How I longed to chase that blush, preferably on her desk as she tried to lay still for me. I shook my head as I pulled up next to Jessica's car in the driveway, ~~driving~~ into the garage. The 22-year-old 'nanny' had been all too easy to convince to stay home, letting me do the pickup today. In fact, she had been so eager, it made me wonder if-

"Oh *fuck*, yes, yes, *yes!*"

I rolled my eyes and turned the radio up in the car, thankful for Lily's less sensitive ears.

"Here," I fished out my tablet from the glove compartment, checking it had enough battery before I gave it to her. "You can have a bit of screen time before we go inside, alright sweetie?"

Lily's eyes brightened, and she immediately put on her favourite game. Within seconds, she was zoned in, and once I was sure she wouldn't hear anything, I went into the house, leaving her in the car.

As I made my way through towards Jessica's room, the cries only got louder, more desperate and keening. Frankly, they rose so high in pitch, I almost worried for her vocal cords. I brushed past the barely closed door and smirked at the sight.

Jessica was bent like a pretzel, folded almost in half, her eyes rolled so far back I doubt she even saw me enter. Her blonde hair was strewn across her face, drenched in sweat, barely moving as her body jolted from the force of the cock slamming into her pussy. A line of drool had begun to crust alongside the other fluids caked in her hair, the sheer volume of which made me wonder just how long they had been at it.

A fresh drop of come made its way down her tiny tits, joining the pool just under her neck, where it was slowly inching its way down towards the mattress. By the look of things, the live-in nanny had been most certainly 'lived in- no doubt by the end of the month, Emilia would be looking for a new nanny as this last drilling was sure to plant a child in the young ~~fertile~~ woman's womb, if it hadn't happened already.

I looked up at the culprit, her raven hair an almost perfect match to mine, but for the length. The closely cropped locks had a long swooping side fringe, currently matted to the side of her head, where sweat caused it to appear almost blue under the sunlight streaming in from the open windows. *They didn't even close the blinds.*

As sharp lips chewed together in concentration, focused on keeping the brutal pace she inflicted on the girl, large slender fingers made their way down towards Jessica's spread legs. One pried her legs open even wider as the other dipped first into the pool collecting at her neck, before smearing it somewhere below her pistoning hips. Judging by the ensuing wails, she must have found the right spot.

I coughed pointedly, and Ariana's emerald eyes flashed up to mine. She smirked at my unimpressed gaze.

"Pick up go okay?" She huffed out between pumps.

"Oh yes, that's why I'm back with your *niece* waiting in the car, as her nanny helps herself to a nice *cock,* instead being of balls deep in my own juicy twat." I scoffed.

Ari didn't even slow down.

"Just give me a sec, I'm almost done. I can feel this one taking already." She sounded almost proud of young Jessica, for welcoming her seed so readily.

"By all means' take your time *hermana,* it's not as if Lily needs to be in her own home." I walked up to the nanny, who was too stunned, whether from my appearance, or from the force of Ariana's thrusts, to do much more than huff out quick breaths during pumps. "How long has it been, Jessi?"

Her brown eyes pooled with tears as she neared another climax, no doubt overstimulated.

"I- don't – knooow," she wailed as she crested. Ari only doubled down, folding herself on top of Jessica, her breasts, large as cantaloupes, smothering the young women, who found herself huffing around a mouthful of tit, as another engulfed the side of her face. The angle change must have hit something perfect in Ari, as she let out a satisfied groan as her hips flexed, pushing more of her sperm deep inside Jessica's womb.

 I wrinkled me nose at the smell, grateful for the open windows, and made my way out, heading back towards my oblivious niece. Over my shoulder, I called out, "I called it, she's a screamer, you owe me a fifty!"

Honey

All the way home, as I navigated the quiet roads, all I could think about was Alicia. Her eyes, her lips, her *body*, cloaked as it was under the thick material. Sometimes it was innocent, a light observation about the way her hair fell so perfectly around her shoulders and framed her face. Other times, it grew a little dirty, like the way her ass flexed where mine couched- as in, enveloped anything it bumped into. More than one time have I made something disappear underneath my fat ass. The kids find it funny, the other teachers make their snide comments, and I try not to die of mortification.

But I bet Alicia's never made number blocks vanish, at least, not unless she wanted them too? She seemed like the type to explore things, sexually. I wondered if she had ever been with a woman.

Her body seemed like a dream, and truly, many a person would happily lay down beneath her as she stepped on us in her Nike sneakers. I grew a little damp at the thought, and banged my head coming out of the car just imagining her feet, stepping out of the shoes, and onto my chest directly. She didn't seem like the type to heels, yet I was sure her toes would be freshly painted. *wear*

This probably violated a thousand teaching rules and policies, but I comforted myself with the thought that nobody would know. There was absolutely no one to monitor me here, in my own *three* one bedroom home, so instead of shamefully ducking my head and trying to enjoy Friend's reruns, I poured myself a glass of wine, peeled myself out of the blue blouse and slipped off my bottoms, leaving me naked but for my panties, and slightly buzzed after draining the glass in three large gulps.

I topped up the glass and stumbled over to my bed in the corner of ~~the small bungalow,~~ *my room* taking care not to trip over the morning mess I made on my ~~way out.~~ *to work.* Unfortunately, my cheap boxed wine carried more alcohol than flavor, and I fell over my open dresser, landing in front of my wardrobe door.

"Great, real classy," I muttered to myself as I tried to get my bearings. I glanced up at my reflection in the mirrored doors. Full cheeks, a soft brow above dark bushy eyebrows shadowing my large blue eyes. My nose was fine, but my mouth…overly full, with teeth that were just a little too large for my face. My ex once said I resembled a bunny. I always thought it was cute, a fun little pet name. Of course, the day he told me I nearly bit his penis in half with my 'chompers', I learned that he never saw it as a positive.

I shook myself out of my thoughts as I contemplated the rest of me. Despite having a medium small build, my breasts were large, and still somehow plump enough to get me the occasional free drink on those rare nights out with the other teachers. My stomach was soft, with a small pouch that rested gently above my cotton briefs. I tried to imagine it rounder, full of life, how it would swell with a child of my own. How I longed for it.

The wine had spilled on my when I fell, and it now stained the crotch of my panties, as though I were a virgin bride showing signs of her deflowering. I leaned against the side of my bed, using it to help me lift myself enough to remove them entirely, leaving me bare. I was completely smooth, having just waxed last weekend. I was hopeful that I'd get to see some action sometime soon, but so far, nothing.

I was surprised to see my labia puffy and glistening despite no stimulation. Well, no physical stimulation. *Yet.* Thoughts of Alicia's lean muscles caused a soft rolling sensation in the pit of my stomach, and I found my hand trailing down my neck, towards my swelling bud.

How would those hands hold me? Caress me? My other hand found my breast, gently rolling it, before lightly grasping my hardening nipple. *Would she be gentle?*

Or...maybe, a little – rough? I pinched myself and felt my insides clench. *Does she like to be in charge?*

I reached my straining bud and gave myself a rough flick in punishment for being too eager. *Maybe she likes to be pampered? A woman like her must be used to men fawning over her.* My thoughts turned to how she liked to cum. Almost without permission, my fingers slipped into my eager snatch, and I immediately clenched hard around the pair currently knuckle deep. *I bet she can take more fingers.*

Her cunt is probably perfect.

My breath hitched roughly, and my fingers began to move, first gently, in time with the fantasy in my head, then with a mounting desperation. I could feel the crest mounting, higher and quicker than my previous solo sessions, when the wet sound of my fingers pierced through the fantasy. I was embarrassed by the squelching, the thick slick that dripped steadily from my pussy with every curl of my fingers, my body desperately preparing for something I couldn't provide.

As always, I felt myself slowly being drawn out of my lustful haze, until an image of Alicia's gorgeous lips flashed across my mind. How *perfectly* they'd wrap around my nether lips, or her silken tongue wrapping around my eager little nub the same way they did those vowels when her accent came through.

"Come, *querida*," she'd whisper, and like the obedient girl I was, even in my imaginings I flushed hard before I felt that budding crest barrel into me. I let out a pathetic squeak as my body seized and I felt myself gush past my pruney fingers.

When the dizziness passed, I was left mortified by the sheer amount of slick I produced. My last one-night stand had called me up the next day, not for a coffee and repeat, but to send me a dry cleaner's receipt after I 'ruined' his wife's leather sofa. I'd spent the remainder of my lunch trying not to cry and die of humiliation as he talked me through entering his bank details.

His wife could be heard asking how his 'work friend' could have spilt an entire bottle of oil as I hung up.

I morosely eyed the wet patch under me and closed my eyes against that charming memory.

I bet Alicia gives a graceful moan when she comes. And she probably doesn't ruin carpets with her golden syrup snatch.

Alicia

Somehow Lily remained none the wiser about her nanny's extra-curricular activities and was easily brought in for a teatime snack until her parents got home. Ariana headed out after a few minutes joking around with her niece, citing a work event I knew well enough that she was avoiding Emilia, Lily's mother, and I couldn't blame her- in the last year or so, Emilia had started behaving a little *strangely*, so much so even Enrique had noticed, and while I love my brother, he is far from the sharpest tool in the shed.

While he had his own theory of work stresses and the mood swings of life post 'the Change', Ari and I had our own theory; Emilia was getting broody. And with a young fertile woman in the home, she was seeking attention in the worst ways. Ari had already caved in once, but I knew she still felt guilty about the betrayal and had no plans to revisit that chapter of her life.

I personally was amused by the whole thing, but I was also aware that this could be the final nail in the family coffin as it were. We'd all barely survived the blowout with our 'parents' the first time around.

I watched a shaky-legged Jessica maneuver around the kitchen, eventually putting dinner together, as I helped Lily with her math. Help is a bit of an overstatement, she was flying through the exercises, proving just how great a teacher Miss Honey was. Just another reason to love her, I suppose.

As the sound of cars pulling in filled the quiet kitchen, I began to get my stuff together. As much as I loved spending time with Lily, the brief encounter with Honey this afternoon really sparked something in me, and the display Ari put on earlier only revved me up further. It was time for me to go home and 'empty the tank' as it were. I made a quick stop to the bathroom as I heard the door open, and voices filling the house with the sound of fervent discussion.

In the pale blue room, I did my business, washing my hands and trying to see myself as Honey would. I was 6'1 to Ariana's 6'3, both of us towering over Enri's 5'8 build. While Ari was the gym rat, I still boxed, swam and ran in the mornings, giving me broader shoulders than most women, tight muscles across my frame, and an ass that could crack branches off of trees. Of course how she would be able to *see* that beneath the sweats and hoodie was beyond me, but they were necessary- my broad chest muscles made my breasts pop out, and anytime I even *thought* of Little Miss Sexpot, my nipples grew so hard Nasa could use them as honing beacons. Not to mention the *downstairs* situation.

Still. I could try to be more dressed up, and less Hobo-Joe's cousin.

My face did all the work most of the time anyway. I knew my eyes, large, almond shaped and ringed by full lashes, did the entrancing before eyes made it anywhere else. My nose was a perfect blend of straight and angular without appearing aquiline, stopping perfectly above my cupid's bow. My lips, plush and a stunning shade of dusky red, a gift from my Latina heritage I assumed. All this, coupled with my dark waves made me an extremely attractive woman, and that I knew all too well. Surely there was enough to tempt a certain demure madame to my bed for just a little while?

I couldn't be certain of her sexuality, not that it made a difference really, that was the beauty of my situation, but still. It would make it easier for me to judge how to approach her, how to get just a little *taste…*

"Ali, is that you in there?"

Enri's voice cut through my musings, and I shut off the still running water before making my way out.

Enrique

~~Enri~~ and Emilia were both in their mid-thirties, however only Enri showed his age. You would never guess his Latino ancestry from his coloring, blond and pale, run ragged by his corporate job working at Fortuna Majoris. His large brown eyes peered up at mine from behind thick glasses. Lily was perched on his shoulders, clutching his ears.

"Hola Enri," I greeted him with a hug as I hadn't seen him in some time- work kept him busy and away from home often. "How's work going?"

"Oh, same old, nothing new," he said into my shoulder.

"*Really?*" I drew back, raising my eyebrow. "I heard from Ari that there's a promotion up for grabs, with a certain *someone* at the front of the line." Honestly, sometimes it's like he forgets Ariana works at the same office, albeit in a different department, a couple of floors above his.

Enri flushed lightly. "Well, *yes*, there's that, but-" He adjusts Lily's drowsy frame on his back and frowns towards the kitchen, where Emilia can be heard asking Jessica about her day. What a conversation to be a fly on the wall... for

"- to think about it, and I don't want to accept it." Enri continued.

My eyes snapped back to his.

"You don't? I hear everyone wants that role, more money, less office hours- what's not to like?"

"It's not that it's a bad opportunity, of course not, but, in truth, " Enri stammered his way through the sentence. "I only feel they want to give me the job because- because-" He leans in. "Because of *Lily.*"

I blinked down at him. Of *course* it was because of Lily.

In a world where the birth rate is dropping dangerously low and fertility rates are dropping like flies, anyone who have kids below the age of fifteen are highly favoured. In the years since Lily's birth, the Lottery's went from a two-bedroom apartment in the inner city, to a four-bedroom home in the suburbs with a two-car driveway *and* garage. Not to mention the *forest* they call a garden. *Honestly*, I think, staring at Enri with a confused expression. *Did you think your data marketing skills were* that *impressive?*

"Right, so- you're thinking about turning it down?" I asked.

"I already did," he whispers, and my eyebrow shoots up before I can contain myself. Enri is far from a 'go-getter' but still; he's never been a 'no-thank you' kind of guy either.

"Don't tell Emilia, Ariana's probably already heard, but tell her not to mention anything either." He smiles up at me, a wry side smile. "She didn't know about the promotion in the first place, and well- what she doesn't know won't hurt her, right?"

I must have nodded, as when I blinked, he was heading up to Lily's room. I made my way back to the kitchen

Oh Enri. If only you knew.

Emilia Lotteria (or Lottery, as everyone said instead) was a gorgeous woman. Her parents were Sicilian, or at least one was. She was tall for a woman, of equal height to her husband, but very slender, tanned willowy curves wrapped in the finest Italian fabrics a 200k promotion could afford, and looked every bit a European diva. Her blue eyes complemented her blonde pin up curls, pixie nose and red painted lips perfectly.

She could probably still get carded at bars if she wore jeans and sneakers. Instead, I watched her four-inch stilettos cut across the mahogany floors of the kitchen, nary a wince or frown to belay the pain she surely must've felt wearing those all day.

Currently, she was talking Jessica through the itinerary for Lily's weekend, starting as soon as school finished tomorrow. I perked up at the sound of that. No pick-up, perhaps I could drop her off instead? Convince a sweet little miss to come to mine for drinks instead of whatever teachers did in their spare time.

"Oh, Alicia, I didn't realize you were still here." Her melodious voice dropped an octave as she quickly glanced behind me, frowning a bit when the shadows didn't produce another Latina giant.

No Ari for you.

Her eyes slid back over to mine and shooed a doe eyed Jessica away as you would a fly.

"That'll be all, Jessica, thank you." She *click-clacked* her way over to me, her legs crossing perfectly with each step. Her arms slid around mine. Only then did I realize they were still bare from my bathroom perusal. "Come, sit with me for a bit. Enri's gone to Lily to bed, but we both know he'll be in bed in the next ten minutes. So," she said as I sat at the kitchen table, her arm sweeping up my bared arms. "I hear Ari was here before you got home." Her eyes meet mine, steel behind the enticing blue. "What was she doing? Jessica wasn't clear."

Bingo. Emilia was a bit of a bloodhound with things like this. I wonder if she recognized the dick-dazed gleam in Jessica's eyes, or maybe she caught a familiar sniff?

"We were supposed to meet to pick up Lily, a bit of a surprise, with her in the city so much."

"Oh," Her nails dug into my wrist. "Was she waiting long? Jessica said they spoke for a bit."

I scoffed internally. *Oh yes, there was talking, but not from the lips you'd presume.*

"Probably not, I texted her when I went straight to the school instead." I shrugged. "She probably left soon after." I hoped Lily hadn't said anything.

Emilia nodded, and her legs uncrossed as she stood. I raised my eyebrows as she came to stand over me.

"So," she starts, her hands now finding their way to my hair. I really should have left with Ari.

"Anyone new in your life, Ali-cat?"

I coughed. "Not for the moment, no. But you know," I shrugged. "I've got time."

Her eyes tightened. She let out a small laugh. "Yes, I guess you do. You're only, what, twenty-five?"

My eyes widened. Nowadays, you didn't ask girls their age unless they were clearly above forty or for medical reasons.

" A bit younger, I'll never tell," I laughed it off, still stunned at her daring. Fifteen years I've known her, and she still surprises me.

"Oh, I'll get it out of you," she cocked an eyebrow with a challenging smile. "But even so, aren't you worried about-" Her voice dropped even lower. "Your fertility?"

For a moment, there was silence as I contemplated how to even respond to that.

No, I'm not concerned, hyperfertility is practically ingrained into my DNA it seems, if history is anything to go by.

I snorted. If I said that, I'm sure she'd mount me before I'd even finish my sentence. I settled for a half truth.

"Not really, I mean, you and Enri did well with Lily, so I'm sure I'll have plenty of time."

She appraised me silently. "I did do well," she whispered, leaning into me, her eyes darting down towards my lap. Thankfully, there was no response whatsoever.

"I held her seed, carried our baby so well, so *good*." Her breath left her in a rush as a daze overtook her. "It was so hard, to lay there and let him rut, I was so worried about what it would do to Lily, but I was *so* good." She suddenly snapped out of it, as it realizing what she'd admitted, and to *whom*.

My lack of response seemed to embolden her.

"I can be *good* again."

And that was my cue to leave. I stood abruptly, gave her a side hug as I made sure my keys were in my pocket. My phone was in my car anyway.

"Well, it's getting late, Ems, I'll catch you later, okay?"

I slid past her before she could respond. I waved to her silhouette in the garage doorway as I left.

Only in the safety of my apartment did I relax. *I guess she's tired of waiting for Ariana.*

I decided to skip dinner, instead heading to the bathroom. As the water heated, I sent Ari a quick text.

- *She's obsessed.*

who –

- *Who else?*

jess ;) -

- *No, although yes her too.*

lol, it's over there -

- *Does she know that?*

I waited for her response, but there was none. Steam started to fill the room.

- *She just told me she can be good.*
- *Very good*

-     *Again.*

When no response came though, I shrugged and began undressing. A quiet ping came through.

I smirked.

good girls don't beg –

they listen to their master –

and she was never good –

I thought that was it, but a final one come in.

naughty slut -

With that, I switched off my phone, knowing that was her last word on the matter. In truth, it was a more revealing confession that she probably intended. Ariana always had a thing about control. She was the middle child as it were, not that you'd know from her behavior.

She liked her lovers on the submissive side, quiet and unassuming, where she would work them up into a frenzy. The affair already confused me, but this, even more so.

But anyway, that was her lot, at least someone got what they wanted. I stepped in the shower, adjusting the temperature as to not scald my *sensitivities*, and immediately reached down, grasping my dick with a strong grip. It was a little over eight inches, longer than Ari's, although her's was girthier. If that weekend skinny dipping was anything to go by, we both had Enri beat, not that he knew that little tidbit.

Ari and I spent many years growing up comparing and monitoring. Afterall, girls with dicks are hardly jumping out of boxes. There was each other to ask, or the internet, which kept redirecting us to intersex and transgender sites. While the former came close, we were neither really. Porn was surprisingly more accurate- of course the Japanese found a lovely name for us- *futanari*. We have pussies, we have clits, we have cocks. Off course, only the rarest also have-

I clasped my thick balls in my other hand and began moving my hand along my length. *These*, I thought to myself, *these are what the world needs.* Hyper fertile testes that impregnate but also ramp up my internal hormones to the point where I myself could be impregnated successfully. I'd never had the inclination to do either, at least until recently, but I suspected the Change wouldn't affect me.

Or maybe it would affect only *part* of me. Afterall, Ari was 32 and showed no signs of slowing down in any case. I was sure Jessica was pregnant even as we spoke.

The thought of Jessica expecting made me think of Honey, and before long, I was caught up in another fantasy, a favourite of mine- our first encounter. Only, in my dreams, instead of grasping her knitted hips and gently rocking her loose from her cramped position, running out afterwards as to not let my member make a tent in my Christmas dress, I pushed up that skirt, exposing what I'm sure were very demure panties.

I wouldn't even take them off, I wouldn't talk, wouldn't dither about with fingering her little cunt, just two fingers to grab a taste as I shoved myself home. I'd keep her there, motionless as I sucked her juices off of my hand, before thrusting till she no longer knew what was up or down. I'd keep her in that perfect breeding position, humping till my nuts emptied straight into her womb, thumbing her clit to get her walls milking me.

Then, I'd tug her panties back on straight, and wipe my cock on her skirt after fixing it, and she'd thank me for it.

That was always the best part. Her gratitude. *Fuck*.

I came with a stuttered curse and let my come rinse off of me, watching as it swirled down the drain.

Soon, I promised myself.

I can be patient.

I can be good.

Honey

The alarm went off, jolting me from my dreams. I quickly swiped for my phone, tapping the stop button, rolling over as I tried to stop the ringing in my head. That third glass was a big mistake, but I needed encouragement before cleaning up after my release. Speaking of, I grimaced as I felt the damp sheets beneath me. *And that's another laundry load to add to the list of chores for this weekend.*

I couldn't bring myself to feel too bad, the dream itself had been delicious. It was a memory, from the day of the Christmas show, from when I was searching for that bauble, but instead of Alicia helping me out and disappearing afterwards, she tugged down my panties and proceeded to eat me out like it was her last supper. Judging by the puddle beneath me, I'm pretty certain came untouched, simply from the mental stimulation.

This is becoming an issue, an obsession. She probably has a rich fiancé waiting for her in a fancy black car, but here I am wetting my sheets over a woman who probably doesn't even think twice about me.

I took a quick shower, washing and blowing out my hair. It was the worst thing for my curls, but I couldn't bring myself to care. One more day till the weekend, and while I love my students, I was feeling more drained than ever before.

I tugged on my regular cotton briefs, but my eyes caught on a small bag hanging by my dresser. I reached over and pulled out the lacy set my cousin had put in her bachelorette gift bags. I never had an occasion to wear it, but for some reason, the bright blue caught my eye. I decided to wear them, the bra a cup smaller than my usual size. My breasts looked almost obscene, but I figured my cable knitted dress would have a high enough neckline to cover it.

Checking myself out in the mirror, I couldn't help but admire the cut of my ass. Still too large, too soft, but with the lace separating each cheek, it looked perkier than usual.

I quickly packed my bag and made my way to the school. I parked in my allocated bay and made my way to my class through the school corridors, as the outer gate was still closed.

"Morning sweetie," a slimy voice called out. I sighed, knowing who it was and feeling way too hungover to deal with his shtick.

"Good morning, Robert."

Robert Daly- Tall, thin with a balding spot and convinced he was a 'certified breeder' because he and his ex-wife had a set of thirteen-year-old twins. Ever since his divorce, and honestly, even a little bit before it, he had begun hitting on me with increasing vigor.

"You look extra sweet today, Honey, you looking to spread a little *shuga* today?" He smirked. "Because I've got quite the sweet tooth."

I didn't know what to say to that, so I gave an awkward smile and continued to my class.

"Drinks after work, it's on me!" He called out.

"I've got plans!" I tossed over my shoulder. I prepped my classroom quickly, restocking pens, organizing the book corner and setting up their morning activities. I was setting up the monitor when a knock came at the door. In walked the teacher in next door's class, Susan Somerson. Her features were pinched, her hair pulled back strictly from her face.

"Hi Jane," she started. "I wanted to talk about your classroom actually."

"Of course, is everything okay?" I asked.

"Not really. A couple of us have been talking, and we feel it's just a little too out there."

I could feel my self-imposed high from this morning draining rapidly.

"What exactly is the issue?" I asked her.

Susan closed the door behind her with a soft click, and stood by one of the tables, her arms folded tight against her chest. She regarded my walls and table set up for a moment before speaking.

"Your classroom," she began, her voice measured but edged, "is… a bit much. All those colors, lights, and themed corners — it's overstimulating. That's not good for the children's development."

I felt like I was somehow imagining this. I turned, just enough to meet Susan's eyes.

"My kids are thriving," I said evenly.

"The studies of the last decade or so have all shown that overstimulation slows down their learning, not mention that repeated exposure could trigger all sorts of hormonal imbalances, which you *know* is a terrifying thought. That *children* could be subject to this-"

"They're engaged, happy, learning. Isn't that the point?"

"It's not just that," Susan replied, her frown deepening. "You're- you're making the rest of us look bad. Not everyone can — or wants to — put on that kind of show.

The fanfares, with the weekly assemblies, the showcases- last Christmas, the tree and presents-"

"It was *Christmas,* Susan, I was making it festive- "

"And I understand that, but you just take it a step too far. All the parents and students have been raving about it, for months now, and all Sandra hears is 'How will you top Miss *Janey*?"

Surely she's not blaming me *for those enquiries? I had to face them too when* I *took over from* her!

"- She's just miscarried. She doesn't need the extra hassle."

"I'm not trying to make anyone look bad," I answered with a small smile, battling tears. "I just like putting my extra time into my class and students. It's how I show up for them."

Susan's lips pressed into a thin line. "That's not considerate toward the other teachers. Some of us — a couple, actually — have gone through the Change. We don't have that kind of energy anymore. Myself included."

"I understand energy levels change," Honey said softly. "But my choices aren't a judgement on yours." *My own change is approaching fast, don't* I *deserve some measure of consideration?*

The conversation was cut short by the sudden arrival of Alicia, who knocked at the gate. Despite being completely surprised by her presence, I rushed at the opportunity to end the conversation. The door swung open, and she stepped inside, the early sun catching in her hair.

"Oh, hey!" Alicia chirped. "I just wanted to drop off Lily's bottle on my way to work, she nearly always forge—" Her words faltered as her gaze landed on Susan's expression, before flickering back to mine. "Wait. What's going on?"

"Hello, I'm sorry, I didn't know you had a parent meeting this morning- I was just explaining to Jane that she's overdoing things slightly," Susan said. "It affects the rest of us."

Alicia's cheer dissolved in an instant, replaced by a sharper tone. "Excusame, but I've *seen* what she does for those kids. Lily comes home excited, curious, confident. That's not 'overdoing it.' That's teaching. If you're turning that into some kind of accusation, maybe the issue isn't Honey's energy — it's your attitude."

A heavy pause settled in the room. Susan's jaw tightened; she muttered something under her breath and smoothed her pulled back hair. "I see," she said curtly. "I'll leave you two to it."

The door clicked shut behind her, the air seeming to lighten in her absence. Alicia turned back to me, her expression softening into a warm smile. "Don't let that get to you," she said. "The way you care? It matters. More than you know."

I exhaled, the tightness in my shoulders easing. I couldn't help but smile back. Gosh, Alicia's smile — small, but steady — seemingly brightened the entire room. "You said something about water bottles, I think?"

"Si," She pulled out Lily's butterfly bottle from behind her, extending it out to me. I grasped it, our fingers brushing lightly.

"Look," she started, her tone gentle. "I don't know if you have plans or anything afterschool, but if not, why don't you come have a drink at mine? I'm trying out some recipes and, with my sister back in the city and Lily's parents working, I don't have any friends here. I'd love to treat you to a homecooked meal, and all the wine or cocktails you'd like." Her eyes twinkled at me.

Perhaps the Honey of this morning would've refused, but after Susan's words, I just felt exhausted, before the day had even truly started. For once, I stopped considering everything- the students, other teachers, classrooms, the Change, all of it. The only thing I asked myself was if I wanted to go. And looking into her clear open eyes, I said the only thing I really wanted to say.

"Yes, of course."

Alicia

I could hardly believe my luck.

When I found Lily's bottle in the back of my car, I didn't have any thoughts beyond popping in early and *perhaps* getting a coffee together afterschool. But now, she would be in my apartment- on my turf. Oh the possibilities...

Of course, now I had to try putting something together that was not too complicated, but also clearly not takeout. I wasn't a bad cook by any means; although Enri was the master chef in the family, I knew my way around the kitchen quite well. It was just that most of the food ended up slightly harder or softer than it was meant to. Apart from a very select set of dishes, most of the options for *comida en lo de Alicia* came under or overcooked. And I was the better cook of the two sisters, Ariana regularly burned water and scorched pot noodles. *In their pot*. Thank goodness for Enrique, who pretty much kept us alive till we grew financially independent.

I decided to head straight for the store after leaving the school, rather than heading to the gym, where I worked as a fitness coach. It wasn't great money, but it was easy, flexible and, between Enri and Ariana, I knew I wouldn't be left financially dry if things went south anyway.

I sent a hands-free voice note to Marcie, my boss, letting her know I would come in a little later. I didn't have any classes, but there was always something that I could help out with; Being the only real gym in town, *Let Loose* wasn't in a position to hire cleaners and trainers a plenty while simultaneously updating the equipment and facilities.

A she wanted everyone to join, regardless of finance, body type age or gender, Marcella Robbins worked overtime to accommodate everyone in whatever way she could. The result was a stunning – and costly- warehouse renovation that spanned two floors and a basement for mixed -martial arts sparing. She also rented out the space for self-defense classes and occasional shelter for homeless women and children, or domestic violence survivors, as they got back on their feet.

All this meant *I* made peanuts, while helping Marcie juggle all the roles we could. It was a good if hectic system, although she'd been forced to hire two more workers, June and Frances, as Fitness coaches to free her up to manage the accounts more fully after the last eviction warning. Now, the gym was surviving after a large anonymous donation prevented foreclosure, but Marcie had still been looking for an investor.

As I walked into the one superstore in the town, I heard my name being called, that smoky, early-morning voice that always seemed to carry a smirk.

"Well, look who's up with the farmers."

I turned, red basket in hand.

Strolling towards me was my 'boss' and best friend, her honey-blonde hair in two braids down the side of her head, complimenting her tan skin.

"Right back atcha, Marcie. You got my message about me coming in late, right?"

One of her eyebrows arched — her trademark *you're-in-trouble* look. "I did. And what's so important it's stealing you from *Let Loose*'s hallowed halls?"

My cheeks warmed slightly, a rare occurrence, but beside Ariana, no one knew more about my lustful obsession than Marcie, although she didn't know the specifics, as I made sure I was never still long enough for her to get it out of me. But now that things were finally progressing... "I... might have a date."

She straightened, eyes narrowing with interest. "With?"

I busied myself with the tomatoes. "Lily's schoolteacher, Honey Jane. She's come by the gym a couple times." Always in purple lycra shorts, her ass practically swallowing the material. *Fuck,* I loved yoga days. So did my dick.

Marcie's grin widened. "Purple Yoga Lady!" At my raised eyebrow, she continued. "Comes in like clockwork, Tuesday and Friday mornings, although I didn't see her this morning… purple yoga shorts, sweats like she's training for the Olympics?"

She let the words dangle like bait.

"Yep, that's her." I felt the flush refuse to leave me at the thought of *why* she missed this morning's session. "It's not official," I protested. "Just dinner. At mine. One of the other teachers bitched at her classroom being too nice and used 'the Change to try guilting her into being less present for the kids."

Fucking Susan.

Marcie's eyebrows raised in disbelief even as her voice softened for a beat. "What a dick move. I'm nearing the Change and even I don't bring it up." At 30, Marcie showed no active signs of the Change, but it still loomed over her.
"Good for you, Alicia. Dating's not exactly a cakewalk for women like us."

There was that too. Marcie was the only other *futa* I knew of here.

I still remember the shock and panic from when we first realised that about each other, during my 'interview'- a sparring bout after hours. Apparently, my boxing display made quite the impression, and her boxing shorts hid nothing. I was new in town, deciding to move from the city shortly after Lily's birth, and I was going through of a bit of a dry spell. I made sure to grab her plenty of times during the next round, and when she finally had enough, throwing me to the ground and shoving her hands down my sweats, she found the surprise of her life.

While the romantic side of things cooled off after the initial thrill of meeting another *futa* faded, we were still super close in every other way. And when Ari passed her 30th, 31st and 32nd birthday without a cold sweat or hot flash in sight, we all decided to keep each other updated, just in case.

"Do you feel different?" I asked. This was the first I'd heard her speak of the Change in a while.

"I- " Marcie paused as we rounded the vegetable corner. "I *do*, but it's not-" I could see her trying to find words. She leaned in. "I don't get- *hard*- as often. No sudden erections, no urges. It's- *muted* almost."

She looked embarrassed by her confession, but I was concerned. "Is it a lack of external interest? Maybe you're just not interested in anyone? You've basically seen them all, everyone goes to the gym." It's kind of how I felt before coming across Miss Sexpot's phenomenal ass. Marcie shook her head.

"No, I still get wet, there's so many new yoga chicks these days, getting summer ready, I'm almost overwhelmed. It's specifically my little guy. I think he's tapped out. Even when I try a solo session, he's hardly interested."

"Do you think-?" I couldn't bring myself to finish the thought, but Marcie saw where I was going and beat me there.

"I think I'm going through the Change." Her brown eyes met mine, calmly. "I know we theorized that we wouldn't go through it, but I think we do, just- not in the same way. I think Ariana's fem side was neutered, and my masc is going through it now." I shook my head, not wanting to believe it.

"Look, it's just a theory, but in truth, I feel like I imagine a 50-year-old man would- if he went through menopause. The mind is willing, but the body-" She snorts, despite herself. "It's just tired. And it's terrifying because it feels like a part of me is being severed, and I no longer know what to do with myself if it continues. Do I get it cut off? How do I interact with it if I'm fully fem? I'm scared it'll feel like a parasite hanging off of me." Her eyes grew moist, and I rushed in for a hug.

Here I was, fretting about getting my dick wet, when Marcie might be losing it completely.

"It's just a theory Marcie, for all you know, it's stress. It's not like we can ask a doctor; they'd have us dissected by the time you spread your legs." I got a small snort from her. "Look, if this is what the Change means for us, then let's make the most of it. Let's get wasted tonight, I'll call Honey and let her know about the change of plans."

Marcie shook her head fervently. "Absolutely not," she said, drawing away. "Please don't let my self-pity ruin this for you, it's all you've spoken about for months. If *I* can't get some, you definitely should, and Miss Purple Yoga probably has a very juicy snatch if her crotch stains are any indication." She smirked and I rolled my eyes, feeling the air lighten.

"Oh, sincerely hope so, I've been calling her Miss Honey Sexpot in my head for a WHILE. If I can get her pants off, my mouth is the first thing on her." I was quite serious about that; after much deliberation, I'd narrowed it down between my mouth on her, or her mouth on me- *which* me, of course, was up for her to choose.

"Wow, you got it bad. Cunnilingus on a first date as opposed to a quickie on the first surface you find seems an unusual choice for you." I laughed at the reminder of our first time. We went from sparring over a job, to sparring over who got dicked down first.

Spoiler, I won.

"Speaking of unusual… why are *you* here so early? "I asked her.

She tapped her cart handle. "I found a potential silent partner, only he's not so silent. Wants a tour on Sunday. Thought I'd pick up a few bits to freshen the place up. Nothing too overzealous, I'm proud of our gym, sweat stains and all — but a little polish couldn't hurt."

That made me blink. "Since when do you care about impressing some guy? Even for an investment opportunity. The gym's been doing well after that donation, we technically don't need one anymore."

Let Loose had almost been foreclosed in November, too many late payments and not enough paying clients. Marcie had been besides herself and gotten absolutely wrecked on the final day of the notice. A farewell party for closure, she said, which became the theme of the party- 'Forclosure'.

Enri picked us all up- Marcie needed a drinking buddy, and since I was about to be out of work, I had no qualms about volunteering. Ariana helped drag us out, as the only sober one- Marcie wasn't as tall as us, at 5'8, but she was very fit, full of lean, mean muscles, which meant that was *two* crazy large women to wrestle into the car. The next day, as we packed the equipment in silent misery, Ariana walked out of the office where she'd been closing accounts and asked how we'd missed the obscenely large six figure donation sat on our desk. Not only did Marcie pay off the rest of the mortgage, but there was also enough to remodel the place and upgrade it. Sure, Marcie still lived at the back of the gym, and needed to use the bathroom facilities at the crack of dawn before peak times, and *sure,* the money ran out before it could stretch into a payrise for *me,* but it allowed Marcie to hire more help, and now she never had to worry about 'Forclosure' again.

Which is why this silent investor thing confused me. Investors want to change things, that's why Ari suggested the silent route. But now, not only does he sound like a very much talking partner, but he's also gotten Marcie to buy floor polish? Since when?

Marcie gave me a sly look. "Since I decided I could use his money on a new bath *and* shower setup in my apartment." We both laughed at that, rolling towards the checkout together, the air scented with citrus from my basket of limes and a handful of other items I absentmindedly grabbed during our talk.

"So," she said, "what's on the menu for Miss Purple Yoga?"

I froze, looking down at my basket. What *was* the plan? I spied a pack of fajitas at the bottom my collection. "Tacos," I said. Easy choice.

Her lips curved into a slow, wicked smile. "Hope she likes her tacos… hot, messy, and extra satisfying."

I groaned and shoved at her shoulder but couldn't hide my grin. "You're incorrigible."

"And you're welcome," she said, drifting ahead toward the self-checkout, leaving me standing there with the smell of coriander, the sound of her laughter, and a flutter in my stomach and below for reasons that had nothing to do with tacos.

Honey

I have a date tonight! Or, at least, closest thing to it in a while.

I wondered if it was as obvious to the parents and students as I felt it was as I ushered them out with an unusual impatience. Last was Lily, who seemed eager herself to rush into her- I lifted my head to check, and fought disappointment. *No aunt, just her father.* I put false cheer into my voice as I made sure she had her lunch bag.

"What's the plan for the weekend, Lily?"

She beamed up at me. "Mama and Papa are taking me on a trip to the beach!"

Her excitement was infectious, and I smiled as I waved her off, nodding at her father. With that, the class was empty, and with it being the weekend, the cleaners would take care of the classrooms, so I grabbed my bag, checking for my phone. Alicia and I exchanged numbers before she left, promising to text. Just as she said, it was there waiting, sent after lunch.

Hey ;D –

I just wanted to say- don't worry – about what that lady said this morning. You're awesome, the kids are doing amazing (especially Lily!) and frankly, the last thing you need to do is

change –

It's Alicia Padrilla btw –

Then, and hour later-

Oh shit I didn't –

send my address did I –

Here –

See you at 6 ;) –

My smile blossomed into a full grin as I followed the address link. *I shouldn't be this excited for dinner and drinks with* a friend.

I quickly made my way to my car but was waylaid by the principal, who wanted all the teachers to have a quick meeting about the last bout of class trips. I sighed internally, checking the time. I had a couple of hours if I wanted to change, which *yes*, I had paint, chalk, glitter, glue, and what I desperately hoped was slime all over me.

 I took a seat at the back of the staffroom, avoiding eye contact with Susan, Robert and everyone else to be honest. I barely paid attention to the meeting, until my name was called.

"Does that work for you, Honey?" Simons asked. I tilted my head questioningly.

"What was that?"

His eyes darted between me and Susan. "Susan suggested you may be available to lead the June trip."

I refused to look at her. *Old bat.*

Leading class trips was a lot of work in itself, but leading a trip for the *kindergarten*? Not only was it a lot of mental organization and safeguarding checks, but these were *five*-year-olds. In an age where fertility was no guarantee and infant mortality rates were on the rise, if *anything* happened to those children, there would be hell to pay.

I was on the verge of the Change, if the last few months of heat flashes and headaches were anything to go by. I was already far from at my best, my class required a lot from me, but more importantly- *when did I volunteer?*

I had led the every other class trip with minimal support from the others, despite it meant to be on rotation, I even led a first *and* third grade trip, and that was *after* the Christmas showcase that *I* headed.

I was drained.

"I- I don't think that'll be possible Simon, but I thank Susan for the confidence."

"I see, is there any particular rea- ?"

"No, no reason, I'm just not feeling up to it this time." I cut him off with a sweet smile. I didn't want to broadcast my symptoms to everyone, nothing was worse than false sincerity surrounding the Change.

Oh no, are you okay? Did you freeze your eggs? You can always adopt.

The comments specifically from men were even more infuriating. *Are you* sure *it's the change? How can you tell? Maybe it's just PMS?*

I'd seen too many of those conversations to volunteer unnecessary information.

"Ah, okay. No, problem," Simon moved on smoothly. Before long, the meeting was over, and I slipped out before anyone else. This time I made it to my car with no interruptions, and I rushed home, seeing Susan and one of the other teachers leaving the building seconds later.

That was close.

Once home, I quickly showered, shaving and applying a quick mask to my hair. Once done, I applied my favourite apricot lotion, and looked through my lingerie options. *Not* that I thought anything was going to happen, but if I was going to be friends with a woman as stunning as Alicia, I needed to make *some* effort.

I didn't have anything else, so I gave my earlier set a quick sniff. It didn't smell *bad*, just a little musky, which was normal. I walked, ran, sweated, leaked a little discharge. I refused to feel any type of way as I slipped them back on, along with the matching bra. Seeing the mountain of dirt laundry awaiting me, I dug through the back of my closet, spying my green knitted skirt beneath a pile of sweaters. Sure, it was a bit warm for spring, but it was slim pickings tonight. I paired it with a white half shirt from the last parent-teacher meeting and a simple pair of flats. *My* feet were uninteresting. *Hers…* I hoped her flat was a shoes-off kind of place.

Checking the time, I saw I had enough time to grab a bottle of wine before I headed over, and twenty minutes later, I was buzzed up into the apartment. I eyed the brown door, trying to relax as I felt flutters in my stomach, and feared throwing up at her place. What a way to ruin things. Suddenly the door swung open, and I was staring at a truly spectacular chest, highlighted by the cream vest she wore. I quickly looked up and felt those flutters return full force. *Fuck, she was gorgeous.*

"What are you doing outside, silly," she laughed and waved me in, her hair in a simple ponytail. As I my eyes followed the ponytail, I almost missed it when she next spoke.

"Oh, and shoes off, por favor, I have carpet and heated floors, so you should be good."

My brain stuttered to a halt.

Wait.

My eyes slowly slid down, my breaths picking up, her stunning eyes, thick hair, pert breasts, past slender hips, past her -*shorts!*- past her long tones honey brown legs, till they came to a stop on her feet, nestled in the nutty brown of her carpet. Gorgeous, smooth, shapely nails tipped in white.

My breathing stopped completely as my brain fired out one thought.

I want those...in my mouth.

My face flushed an almighty red as my breathing kicked in, and my eyes shot up, hoping she hadn't noticed my silence.

But as I looked into her smirking eyes, I realised, not only did she notice, I think she knew *exactly* what I was thinking.

For what I'm sure won't be the last time tonight:

Fuck.

Alicia

Oh, my dirty little sexpot. Who knew.

I turned and headed for the kitchen, making sure to flex my feet as I did so, hearing her breath catch as she followed.

Your secret is most certainly not safe with me.

Little Miss Honey is into feet. I felt my dick stir as I wriggled my toes into the carpet. *Oh, the possibilities.* I poured her a glass of wine and held it out, waiting on her to make the first move. She reached out hesitantly, her face still aflame. Our fingers brushed and a rush of heat flared up between us. She quickly took a gulp of wine as she drew away, choking slightly. I smiled as she took in the room for the first time.

I had something of a green thumb and made sure to flex it often. Potted trees filled the corners of my apartment.

Fortunately, my apartment faced the sun, and being on the third floor, I felt confident enough leaving the windows bare, ensuring they received plenty of sun. winding plants climbed my shelves, which were pretty bare. A couple of photos of Lily and a few childhood photos with Ari and Enri. She stepped closer to see them.

"Oh, these are so cute," she exclaimed, reaching out to take a closer look. "I can see the family resemblance."

"I'm told it's all in the eyes," I responded absentmindedly, ensuring dinner was ready.

"Ooh yes, but- oh wait." Her tone made me glance up and my eyes narrowed slightly. She held a picture of the three of us as kids and was closely peering at it. "Is that your sister?"

"Yes, Ariana." I wondered what was going on in her head.

"Lily looks a lot like her. Especially the eyes, my goodness." She looked back at me. "Although, her hair is much brighter. That's a beautiful shade."

I hummed. "Most of the people have dark hair in our family. Enri is a bit of an outlier."

I heard her step closer as I spoke, shrugging out of her jacket. "I saw on Lily's family tree that there were no grandparents on your side of the family."

I felt my shoulders tighten, but I shrugged it off as best as I could. This evening was about us getting to know each other after all. Still, I had specific plans for the evening, and I didn't want to spoil them by clamming up about our 'parents'.

"That's right, we're not in contact with them anymore." I finished plating everything up before gesturing for her to take a seat. The shirt she wore gaped a little at the top and it provided a lovely picture to go with the meal.

"I don't mean to- well, I *do*, but it's more of a conversation starter. Please don't feel you have to elaborate." I appreciated her honesty, and to be frank ~~myself,~~ I would confess all for a glimpse more of the ᵛᵉˣ cleavage.

"It's okay, there's not *much* to tell. Our birth parents died when we were quite young. With three of us, placements together were nearly impossible at first. Enri was placed with our parents first, while we stayed at a foster placement." Aunt Lorna turned out to be a futa, which was of great help to Ariana, who had started going through puberty early. That was a futanari trait, as we have two sexual organs to mature.

Unfortunately, she was quite old and passed before my own puberty. Ari was old enough to recognize that she and now I, were unique in a sense, and that this wasn't something to share with others. So, by the time the parents came for us, we were already washing and dressing ourselves, Ari at twelve, me at four. "We picked up some habits from Aunt Lorna, which gave us a bit of trouble when we were finally adopted."

We began to eat as I spoke, and I was proud of myself for not messing it up in anyway. Evidently Honey agreed, judging by the sounds she made after the first bite. I found myself transfixed for a moment.

"What kind of habits?" Her cheeks puffed in the sweetest way, and my dick began to stiffen as I envisioned filling them with something else.

"Nothing crazy, or extreme. We took showers together," I swallowed a mouthful of beef, red onions and avocado topped with chili sauce. "Not together exactly, but at the same time. While I washed, she brushed her teeth, and vice versa. We didn't go swimming in anything but t-shirts and trunks, no matter how hot it was. Or we wouldn't sleep in different beds until I was thirteen. It drove our parents crazy."

"What, why? That's sounds adorable, you guys were so close."

Well, yes, but we *had* to be. Ari was very careful in never leaving me alone with either parent or even Enri, to risk them finding out about us. While my dual organs weren't on show yet, so I could wear panties and speedos with no concern, Ari felt it was safer just in case I suddenly *did* start to show. There would be less questions about the transition if we were already conservative, which she was, having been well in the thick of it at the time.

"I don't know if it was an intimacy they were denied, or if it just annoyed them how self-reliant we were overall. Anyway, Enri was fine with it, never bothered him, so in time, we regained that familial bond. However, our relationship with our parents grew worse. Our father thought we had some great secret, like stock bonds in our underwear or something, so he raided our closets and dressers whenever we were out.

When that provided nothing, he moved on to every imaginable hiding place in our room, and eventually Enri's room, and the rest of the house." Honey's blue eyes were horrified, but bless her, she kept eating. *Good girl. Ariana was on to something there.*

"While our father grew paranoid, our mother seemed determined to gain that deeper relationship, not understanding that the more she pushed-"

"The more you pulled away." Honey finished quietly. I met her eyes, sensing her own story.

"Indeed. She had removed all the locks in the house, all curtains before we'd even been adopted, yet we made it work because we still had doors. And Enri, little genius, figured out how to block them, top and bottom, for secure privacy, showed us how to do it. When she realised Enri had found ways around that, she removed them too. Everything was open. It was a nightmare."

"I- I can't even understand why a parent would *do* that?" I shrugged at her and took a sip of wine. She mirrored me.

"We'd decided to move out as soon as was physically possible. We didn't have many, if any friends. We'd grown so used to clamming up at home that we found it hard to undo it in high school. Then the Change started affecting more and more women, and something seemed to click in our father's head. Here we were, humanity facing a fertility crisis, and he had three young teens under his roof." Despite the calm in my voice, I felt my hand tremble slightly at the memory. I dimly noticed Honey placing her glass down firmly.

"He-he- didn't-surely *not-*"

"He tried, with Enri. With Ari. He invited people over, hoping to have *something* happen. But by then, we had taken to sleeping all together in the same room. We made a fort, and we all slept together, so you couldn't get one without the others there. Enri was seventeen and working out, Ari was already 6' at fifteen."

"Please tell me that's it. You moved out as soon as Enrique turned 18?"

"Not exactly. I was only seven, they couldn't take me anywhere without a police red alert following them. And applying for guardianship was going to be difficult as we were legally theirs, not wards of state. So instead of leaving, they stayed. Enri went to the local community college, got his marketing degree. Met Emilia, but he stayed home till Ari was eighteen. Then he proposed, got married, started staving and got a local apartment.

Ari was a different story. She was bright, *is* bright, and it was clear she was destined for an Ivy-League school, or some crazy internship straight out of high-school. But I was thirteen, still a little too young for the runaway scene."

I focused on my drink, feeling Honey's eyes on me. This really wasn't a romantic story, but it was hard to stop once the ball started rolling.

"Our parents pushed for her to go, she had scholarships to so many universities, and head-hunters were keeping an eye on her. But she couldn't leave me. She deferred indefinitely, during which time Enri got married, she took several remote admin gigs to pass the time and make money, some of which she presented to our parents, the bulk of which she kept in savings.

When I was fifteen, the plan was to leave at sixteen, and we were a few months shy of it. But our mother found the texts between Enri and Ari, talking about finding apartments, and plane tickets. At first, they thought Ari was finally going to college, but the Emilia let it slip that I had a ticket to. Something clicked, and my parents all but had Ari escorted from the house by police, claiming they no longer wanted her home. Ari tried to fight them, but the some of the police force had been those same individuals who our father brought round years ago.

There was nothing she could do, so she left for Harvard, found a job at Fortuna and somehow juggled both, trying to save as much as she could to come back for me.

I think there was a plan between the two, where Enri was meant to move back home, but he was married now, and his priorities were split. Emilia was fast approaching the Change, and every year without a child put strain on their marriage. He wasn't as diligent as he should have been, and one night, they caught me in the bathroom."

I left it there for Honey to imagine up the rest. I stood, cleared the plates and headed for the fridge.

"I have cake, if you have room for it," I murmured. She'd eaten more tacos than *me*, which was impressive. I heard a choked noise behind me, and I turned reflexively.

Honey sat with her hands clenched together tightly at the table, tears pooling in her eyes. I closed the fridge in surprise. "Honey, are you okay?" I cursed myself internally for posing such a stupid question. *Of course she's not okay- you just dumped your childhood trauma on her for an hour. She asked* one *albeit nosy question and that was your response. No* wonder *you're single. This night is not going to end how you planned. Moron.*

Honey shook her head, and stood in a rush, making me dart around the table in panic. *Is she gonna leave? Fuck! Say something. Now!*

"Hey, it's okay, nothing happened!" *Whoops.*

"What do you mean, nothing *happened?*" Honey whispered in disbelief.

Yes, what do *you mean?*

"They didn't touch me-" *Much* " And anyway, the story ends with me running away, Ari getting me a plane ticket, and bamn!" I gave a little twirl on the spot, knowing my vest would ride up a little. "Nine years later, my brother and sister-in-law are rich, with a daughter, my sister's at the top of her field in one of the fortune 500 companies and I'm in my own apartment," *Good save.* "- with *doors-*" *Huh?* "- having dinner with a stunning date-"

WAIT

"- who blushes at the sight of my toes."

No, seriously, what. The. FUCK?

Honey was stunned into silence, and I fought the urge to call it a day. Or rather, night. I bit my runaway tongue, vowing to cut it off.

"...date?" Honey whispered.

I winced. "Yeah, so I kinda have a crush, on you, and thought you might be interested in a date. With me. And *this,*" I gestured at the semi cleared table. "Is our date."

Honey's cheeks slowly ripened, a high color red, which would've giving me hope but, I sighed in disappointment, high color can be embarrassment, mortification, *extreme* pity-

Plump lips found mine, slightly chapped from teeth worrying away at them, but deliciously soft all the same. They pressed and released mine, in a sensual pattern that very quickly sent blood draining before my mind caught up to what was happening. All too sudden, those lips pulled away, and I eagerly chased them, my hands reaching for her face.

Fuck, Honey. You precious thing.

Our kisses grew desperate, more fervent, and I felt myself pushing her back, past the chairs, past the table, beyond walls, to my couch. I wouldn't want her to come to her senses in the time it takes to get to the bedroom. I wasted no time in unbuttoning her shirt, one at a time, in an extreme display of patience.

If I rush this, I may never get it again, I thought, and after months of solo pining, I was prepared to savor every part of this. I kissed her jaw, her chin, her neck, slowly moving down each square of revealed skin, until the fabric parted completely, and I sent a quick prayer of thanks to the big guy for my luck this evening. Such gorgeous mounds, held up in a fantastic bra that I at once removed, letting those weights fall into my hand.

I juggled them both in my palms, squeezing firmly as I rolled them around, pressing them into each other as I dropped my head. My kisses rained down on them, and my tongue darted out to catch a taste of her ruby nipples, firm and erect, digging against my tongue. *Fuck, these would look good with milk leaking from them.* Just the thought sent my hard dick into overdrive, and I couldn't help but press my hips into the couch, hoping to ease the pressure momentarily so I could *focus.*

Honey let out a little squeak and I sucked those teats into my mouth, one at a time, sucking hard. She writhed beneath me, her hips undulating wildly as she moaned, and I felt all rational thoughts leave my head. She quickly pushed her skirt down, and I helped her kick them off, pressing a quick kiss to her feet.

I moved one of my hands down her smooth hips, trailing it down closer to her mound, decadently wrapped in lace. When my fingers passed over it, she let out a wail as I made contact with the soaked fabric, and I smiled around the breast in my mouth. I lifted my head up to meet her eyes, the blue orbs practically glowing down at me as she breathed out my name.

"Alicia, *please.*"

I let out a low laugh. "Oh, *Honey,* my sweet girl. You need something from me?"

"Please, *please,* I-" I shushed her gently, as I slowly peeled the wet fabric off down her legs. I made sure to slip them into my pocket for later. She wouldn't need them again anyway. I quickly leaned down to press my lips against hers, my tongue flicking out to grab a quick taste before I made my way to her honeypot.

Oh, fuck. Honey, you're dripping, baby.

"You poor darling. Look at all this honey just waiting for me." I smirked up at her. "It seems a waste to let it just sit there, without getting a taste."

Honey's eyes frowned in confusion, her breaths coming in quick. She opened her mouth, but I quickly ducked down and took a long, lingering swipe at the cunt that had plagued my thoughts and dreams.

My eyes rolled back at the sweet tangy taste of her honey, and I eagerly went in again, dimly aware of Honey's keening cries when I found her nub, swollen and straining towards my tongue. I nibbled, flicked, sucked at her, loving the feel of her quivering labia, twitching with every lick. I brought my hands down to play, one keeping her legs splayed open for my shoulders, gripping the top of her soft thigh, digging into the supple flesh. The other made its way to her dripping snatch, one finger pressing in smoothly alongside my tongue. It sunk in deep, and I had to take a moment to stop the top of my dick from blowing off at the feel of her silken walls.

"So *tight.*"

She let out a whimper, and I felt her clench harder around my finger in response.

"Think you can take two?"

She nodded eagerly, and I chuckled, slipping in another, reaching deep and curling deep, locating that spongey spot and bearing down hard. Honey jolted up, her legs finding their way around my neck, and I fucked her roughly my fingers, drawing out the pleasure as I sucked her bud firmly. She let out a wail as she came, and a gush of slick drenched my hand. I stared at my wrist in shock, as her release soaked into the sofa's light fabric, leaving a large spot. *My little sexpot gushes like a waterfall. Could she be any more perfect?*

"I- I'm sorry, oh my gosh, I'm sorry, I can pay for it-" Honey stuttered out, her face a blotchy red as she gazed at the spot in distress.

"What are you talking about?" I asked her in confusion.

"The- the couch, I'm sorry, I didn't mean to- to make a mess." Her voice broke. "I'm sorry."

I could only stare up at her. "It's not a mess, baby, it's your come. And there's nothing to apologize for, I made you come, and it was my privilege. Why-" I paused at the look on her face. "Baby- did someone tell you that this was something to be ashamed of?"

Honey bit her lip. "My- the last guy I was with. He called me after to- to send me a dry-cleaning bill."

"He- *what?*" I stared in disbelief.

Honey finally began to lose some of her flush as she took in my expression. She laughed slightly. "I mean, I probably shouldn't take his actions to heart, turns out he had a wife, and it was *her* limited-edition designer lounger, I think. He told her a colleague spilt oil on it."

My eyebrow quirked up. "I hope it wasn't virgin oil," and Honey snorted, collapsing fully against the cushions.

"Oh no, that ship sailed a *years* ago. That was a one-time thing, but still. It was embarrassing to get a call back only to hear that your *oil* messed up a 20,000 dollar cushion." I laughed at the wryness in her voice, pressing my face into her skin. A drop of her release trickled down her thigh, and I batted her hand away when she reached down to wipe it away, making her head tilt up to watch me.

"I want you to listen very carefully to me when I say this," I turned my head slightly, and gave her thigh a long, languorous lick, making sure to slurp up that droplet before I met her gaze. "That man was an absolute idiot, who had no idea what to do with a honeypot as good as yours. I bet he didn't even get a sample, did he?" Her face colored and I had my answer.

"You've got a gorgeous pussy, which is both juicy and delicious," I gave it another languid lick when it winked at me. "And I would love to get to know it better."

Honey beamed down at me, before dragging me up to her lips- I was careful not to brush against her, where I proceeded to shove my tongue as far down her throat as possible, feeling her suck, her juices off of my tongue. Fuck, that only made me harder. Which reminded me of a pressing detail I needed to get out of the way.

But before I could do so, Honey panted against my lips, "Now it's your turn," and her hand shot down to grab at my shorts. I backed up in alarm, but her legs coiled around my waist, pulling me into her. I froze when our hips collided, my dick pressing into her core. *Shit.*

Honey's brow's crossed as she tried to make sense of what she was feeling. I was caught between pleasure and pain as I wordlessly stared her, unable to say a word.

"Wait, is that- are you wearing a strap on? Someone was looking to get lucky tonight!" She started giggling uncontrollably, the movements making my dick twitch in response. Her giggles turned to a gasp as she felt the motion. "Woah. Wait, did it move? You can make it *move* like that?"

Her eyes took on a greedy glint. "I was thrilled with where this was going, but I'm on board for whatever this is," she said, lifting herself into me. I winced as I felt pre-come slipping from my tip steadily. The stimulation was too much. I had been hard for this woman for so long that the light rocking was enough to almost make me lose it. I tried to halt her movements.

"Wait, there's something I need to tell you," I tried, but Honey was on the go, finding her pleasure. I grasped her hips, but in a display of strength I didn't expect, she knocked me onto my back and proceeded to grind down on me like she was in a rodeo.

The breath was knocked out of me as I stared up at her, completely stunned by her ferocity. *Where did that shy teacher go?*

She was magnificent, and I found myself rocking along with her. *If this is about to go south, I might as well enjoy the calm before the storm.* I tightened my hold on her and on her next forward grind, I thrust up into her like there was nothing between us. She gave a low keen and stiffened as the first of her release washed over her. I rolled her into the back of the couch and lifted her leg for a better angle, giving short rapid thrusts into her molten heat, her come gushing over my shorts to my dick. I shuddered at the feel of her slick on my dick, even muted through the fabric, and I buried my head into her neck as I came with a moan of my own.

Wow.

Sparks were still firing off in my head, which is why it took me a moment to realize that Honey had stiffened in my arms.

"Hey, everything o-"

I froze. With my enthusiastic orgasm over, my cock had begun to deflate. And with Honey perched on top of me, she sensed the change instantly.

"Uh-"

"Alicia, is that-? Was that real -? Are- are you- a-" Her voice was unsure, and I could sense her searching for the right words. I cut in before she could stumble further.

"I'm not transgender. "

Her face still held a confused look. "So, you're a man?"

"No! No," I exclaimed. "I'm a woman, I just- have a penis."

"Oh, we had a discussion on that during the inclusivity meeting. 'Intersex', I believe it was called."

I winced slightly and sat up. This was a conversation best had with a bit of space. And a possible demonstration. My dick stirred slightly. *Not like* that, I scolded my dirty thoughts.

"Yes, that's a thing, similar to what I am, but not quite." I took a deep breath. "I am a woman. My blood, chromosomes, brain, body proportions- all female. However, I have a fully operational penis, and-" I winced. "Testicles. Theoretically also fully operational."

Honey gaped at me. "You-you can have children?" I nodded. "As in *father* them? *And* carry them?" I nodded again. Then winced again.

"In *theory*. I've seen it done once, but she might be an outlier. And being that my menses are pretty regular, I'm as sure about my ability to carry children as much as any other woman is before trying."

"So how is that different from being intersex?" Honey asked. I scanned her face but found open curiosity. No judgement, discuss, or worse, that hungry gleam Emilia carried in her eyes these days. "If you have both, doesn't that make you a hermaphrodite?"

"In theory yes, but there's a lot of grey spaces with intersex identification, whereas for us, it's pretty straightforward. We're women who also have dicks. Now I'll admit, the testicles are a minor grey area." I paused thinking of Marcie. "I've only met three others like me, and one was that foster placement I told you about. I have no idea if she had testicles as, well, I was a kid, I never saw her naked, but one of the other two don't. The other successfully impregnated a biological female. So, it seems if you have them, they function as usual, if not, then you have the rest, but probably can't breed other women. "

Marcie had no external testicles, but we theorized that she must've had some form of internal ones, as her testosterone level, while not as high as Ari and I's, it was not that far below (and ours were only slightly above the usual amount in women.)

"So, when- *if*- we have sex, you could…get me pregnant? Or wait, has the epidemic affected you too?" Honey blushed as she spoke, and I knew we were both thinking about her earlier slip.

"Yes, that is a possibility. The issues with sperm production don't seem to affect us." I thought back to my earlier conversation. "Although, one of the others have a theory that we go through a Change of our own, which dampens one of our sexual organs."

Honey nodded, deep in thought. I shuddered as I felt my come drying in my shorts, but I refused to stop this conversation till I knew where Honey and I stood.

"Okay, I think I get it now."

She groaned, dropping her head into her hands. "I think I have to be the worst date ever. First, I poke my big nose into your family affairs, then I interrogate you about your- gender? What do I call it?"

I smiled wryly. "I hope you call it my dick, that is its name."

Honey laughed, and I continued.

"We-" I flushed a little at my next words. "We call ourselves futanari. It's not perfect, it has very clear connotations, which are often overly fantastical about it all, but it's better than being directly under the banner of intersex. I don't want people who actually have that to think we are their representatives; we'd be piss poor at it. But we *are* hermaphrodites in the biological sense. We're women who have everything women have, plus a dick, and occasionally, testes. We have periods, we have perhaps a slightly larger build if we have balls- come to think of it, Aunt Lorna probably didn't, she was tinier than you."

I poked Honey and she fell into me giggling. I tentatively pulled her into my arms, pressing a kiss in a hair when her arms slid around mine.

"I know it's a lot to take in. It wasn't- I didn't mean-" I couldn't finish my sentence without making it a lie. "I *hoped* to get to know you like *that* tonight, yes, but not like this. I was going to ease you into it, over probably the next few dates or something, I know it's a lot to take all at once."

"I'll bet it is," Honey snarked, and I burst out laughing. *Dirty girl, you can have it. All at once or in instalments, it's all yours.*

Honey pushed back and pulled me into a soft kiss. I held my breath, not wanting to disturb this moment.

"Look, this was a surprise, a *big* one- but not unwelcome. I told you earlier, I'm all in with you. You're still very much the sexy Latina I've been thinking about nonstop for the past twenty-four hours, and even if that was all you were, I'd still be here, humping you all weekend long. It just turns out there's more to you, and frankly- " Her hand trailed down my still very much overdressed torso and traced her damp patch over my stirring dick.

"I can't wait to explore every inch."

Honey

I can't believe I just said that.

I made sure to look Alicia in the eyes as my hand kept its slow deliberate movements. I could feel her *cock* slowly thickening.

Cock. I almost couldn't believe it; *she had a fully functional dick! And balls, she could, she could impregnate someone, she could* breed *someone, breed* m-

I cut my mental train of thoughts off at the station before it could entice me further into riding this promising length into the sunset like a stallion. Even as my mind battled with itself, my pussy was all on board, I wasn't lying about that. Even when I thought it was a silicone piece, I felt myself drooling in my nether regions. Now that I knew it was a real, hot, *operative* piece of machinery, my pussy was damn near frothing at the lips.

Evidently my vagina was ready to get acquainted with whatever was now pulsing between my hand, and before I knew it, my hands were scrambling at her shorts. She helped me remove them with a low groan, which turned into a loud exclamation when my hands seized her length with a firm grip.

Fuckfuckfuckfuckfuck.

I was screwed.

Her dick was *gorgeous*.

Long, so long it cleared my hands where they gripped him, with room to spare, thick and veiny, protruding from a dark curly bush, tracing up towards a gloriously flared head. I should have been disgusted, *there was still come drying on the sides, for crying out loud,* but all I could think about was tasting her, as she had tasted me. So I did.

"Ungh, *fuck,* Honey," Alica grunted as my tongue laved over her glistening tip. I found the opening slit of her urethra with my tongue, and she bucked wildly into my face, pushing that fat head, and at least a third of her length into my open mouth. I let out a whimper at the sudden intrusion, my tongue almost fizzing at the taste of her.

"Oh fuck, baby! I'm sorry, I'm so sorry, I won't move, your mouth is just so fucking- *fuck!*"

I refused to let her push me back, as she clearly did *not* want to, and so in a preventative move, I tried to make sure my teeth were out of the way before I attempted to inhale her length into my throat, with mixed results.

At first, that bulbous head slid along my tongue with no issues, traversing past my aching jaw, into the base of my throat. Only, the shock of it there, and the thought of- I felt around the base of her- at least another three inches to go made me swallow in surprise. Alicia gave another hoarse shout, and I tried to take a breath reflexively, causing my gag reflex to kick in, and I choked around that absurdly huge cock. *Shit, I can't- how do I breathe?*

Alicia quickly pulled back, but I was determined to finish. I shoved my face right into her crotch, my nose pressing into the soft, wiry bristles. Unfortunately, in my eagerness, I forgot about my teeth, my 'chompers', and I accidentally dug them into her thick length.

"AH- *shit*, ow, wait-" Alicia pushed me off of her, and I fell to the side, my face aflame.

FUCKFUCKFUCKFUCKFUCKFUCK, NOT AGAIN.

Alicia must've sensed my building panic and quickly pulled me into a kiss. I felt hot tears leaking from my eyes, and I tried to brush them away before she saw.

Honestly, Honey, she's the one who nearly lost her dick, why are you *crying?*

"Baby, it's okay, it happens," she started, but I cut her off with a wail.

"I'm so sorry, *shit*, are you okay? I knew I shouldn't have tried, *fuck,* I'm so bad at this, these fat, fucking *chompers-*"

"Hey!"

I blinked up at her in surprise. Alicia wore a stern look on her face.

"I happen to like those 'chompers', don't you ever refer to them like that again." She kissed me again, making sure to give my teeth a lick as we parted. "It takes practice, no one gets it on the first go, and I am more than willing to go again if you are. Look," she drew my attention to where her dark length stood, stretching desperately up towards her navel. "He's more than happy to go again."

I couldn't hide my wince at the thought of biting her again, despite the urge to choke myself on it again. It really was delicious. Alicia noticed.

"Or, if that's too daunting right now," she grabbed my hands and trailed them lower, using one to cup the thick weights of her fuzzy balls. I couldn't help squeezing softly, feeling them warm my hands with the heat of sperm just itching to breed some unexpecting uterus. *Mine.*

Our other hands slid below, encountering a dewiness that caused my breath to hitch. She let my fingers rest there, until I grew inpatient, and slipped them in, the tips of two fingers cutting a path into a silky wetness that made me whimper.

Shit, she was so fucking perfect.

Alicia gave a soft sigh. "There we go. We can start there," she said, closing her eyes as my fingers slid deeper, filling her nicely.

While I had fooled around with girls during college, it had never felt like *this*. Like I would die if I didn't get more of her on me, if I didn't fill her cunt with my fingers, I'd be wasting the rest of my life. I eagerly dropped my head to see, and the sight of her tiny wet pussy, hidden behind her scrotum like a little treasure, was enough to tempt me into getting a taste of her other secretions.

If her come was salty and thick, her slick was tangy and gooey, and I lapped at both, bobbing between her leaking rod and her scorching heat, alternating eagerly. On my fifth pass around her opening, I found her clitoris, swollen in its hood. I flicked my tongue around it, feeling Alicia tremble, and I suckled at it like a nursing kitten. She moaned loudly, her hand shooting down to hold my head in place, my lips working furiously until she came, my fingers lazily massaging her inner walls. As I looked up, feeling proud that I'd managed to make her come, despite my previous blunder, I was surprised by the sight of her cock still straining above me.

"Oh," I said dumbly. Alicia removed her arm from her eyes and peeked down at me, breathing heavily.

Her gaze was dark and predatory, and I swore I felt my womb cramping in response.

" 'Oh', baby? My dick ain't going down till you sit on it. Or bend over, it's not too fussy."

I licked my lips at the thought, and Alicia's eyes darted down, darkening further. She pushed her ring and middle fingers into my mouth, probing around every crevice, every tooth, even dipping into my throat, before removing them. I watched in shock as she reached across and slid them into my waiting snatch, bringing them back to her mouth for a taste.

"I just wanted to get a final taste of your honey, before it's filled with cream."

oh.

I threw myself at her, feeling my core ignite; I tore off her top, revealing her toned teats, and I latched on to the dark bud of her areola, managing to get a squeeze of both breasts before she stood, her dick now bobbing in my face, leaking those big pearly drops. I leaned in quickly, hoping to get my own final taste, but Alicia was quicker. She pushed me down onto the soft rug beneath the couch, shoving a cushion beneath my hips. I gazed up in anticipation, knowing that my life was about to change forever. Heck, it already had.

Alicia crawled over me, hissing as her cock brushed against my dripping pussy. *Wait*.

I was brought out of the moment by how wet I was. *The rug...*

"Wait, Alicia, your rug-"

Alicia chuckled darkly. "Don't worry about the rug, Honey, worry about yourself." She brought the tip of her cock to my entrance, softly rubbing it in my juices.

My pussy clenched, but I couldn't quite shake off the thought of her rug being ruined. I hoped this would be a long-term (maybe forever) thing between us, but if all I got was one night, I would die of mortification if the best sex of my life was followed by a dry-cleaning bill. I tried again.

 "It looks really- delicate, m-maybe we should mo-*move-*"

"It's not nearly as delicate as you, pet."

Alicia didn't even pause in her rocking motion, smoothly inserting that shiny helmet into my tight opening, before popping it out with a wet *shlurp*. Her thumb came to a rest above my clit, thrumming it smoothly, as she moved. I could hardly focus, feeling the warmth building fast.

"It- *ah, fuck*- it looks expensive, I really think- "

"You know what's more expensive, Honeypot? Diapers. And baby formula. Which you're going to need. In nine months."

With that, she slammed home.

OH.

I seized up with an instant orgasm. When my senses came back to me, Alicia was pistoning her cock into me with a feral glint in her eyes. I tried to pull her in for a kiss, but she shook me off, grabbing both my hands and pinning them to the side.

"No, you're gonna keep those right there," she huffed, her hair falling from the loosened hair tie in waves around her face. I whined at the rolling sensations I felt every time that thick, uncut monster of hers dragged against my walls. With my hips tilted, each thrust punched at that spongey center deep inside, and I felt myself clenching once more.

Oh fuck, two? In a row? Judging by the gleam in Alicia's eyes, she was no way *near* finished. *I won't make it. But I'll die happy.*

With my head still spinning from my first orgasm, I barely heard Alicia.

"I'm trying to fuck my little honeypot, like a good bumblebee, but all you can focus on is *where* I should do it."

I opened my mouth to deny it, but she bit my lower lip, sucking it softly when I whined in pain, softening the sting.

"Shhh baby," she crooned into my neck, nipping at my jaw.

"I know some idiot got you thinking shit like that is important, but it's really not. This rug? It's nothing. Means *nothing*. Not when I've finally got you spread open for me, the way I want, the way I've been *dreaming of*."

She released my wrists, lifting my soft thighs onto her shoulder so she could rut deeper into me. The new angle sent frissons of pleasure to my core, and I clamped down on her with my second orgasm, wailing the walls down.

By now the sound of wet clapping filled the room, and I could feel our skin almost fusing together, like our bodies were trying to fuse into one. Alicia gave a quick grind against my bud on each of her next thrusts, and my eyes rolled back as a third orgasm crept up behind me.

Shitshitshit, toomuch, it's too much!

My pussy was so sensitive, it bordered on painful, but Alicia wasn't done yet.

"Alicia…"

"Six months. *Six fucking months*. That's how long it took for you to see me. Six months of waiting, hoping, *pining* like a fucking schoolgirl-" her fast pumps slowed into deep, hard-hitting thrusts that had me trying to crawl away, roll over, anything to escape the sensations that threatened to overwhelm me.

Alicia tutted, and pressed almost all her weight into me, keeping me pinned and fucking me into the floor, my legs by my ears.

Thank fuck for yoga.

"Six months of volunteering for school events only to find out you weren't there, or you were too *busy* to notice me; six months of trying to pick up or drop off Lily while her nanny gets dicked down on the kitchen table- *but you never saw me.*"

I couldn't control the shuddering sobs that left me at her string of revelations. *I could have had this then. I didn't have to be alone. Why couldn't see you?*

"And now, after six *long* months, now that I've got you right here, wet, willing and wanting- you want me to care about a rug? Over *this?*" Alicia gave a particularly deep thrust, and I felt her hit some sort of barrier in me. Flames of pleasure and pain exploded through me, and I gasped up at her in disbelief, feeling caught as that third orgasm remained just out of reach, tears blurring my vision till all I saw was the green glow of her eyes.

Fuck, was that my cervix?

But Alicia was still not done.

"Don't worry darling," she panted as she ducked down to press a lingering kiss against my lips, making her next words wash over me.

"I'll give you a nice baby to look after."

I keened, nodding desperately. *Yes, please, I want one, I want a baby, it's all I ever wanted.*

"Yeah? You wanna carry my baby, Honey? I better breed you right the first time, so we can get started on another straight away. Don't want them to get lonely."

I was so close I was nearing overstimulation. Alicia finally seemed to near her own peak, picking up the pace once more.

"And then -*fuck*- when you're carrying our beautiful babies, I'll ask you to marry me, we'll get our dresses on and make it official, 'kay baby? *Shit*, you'll look so pretty, my sexy little honeypot, my baby mama, fuck, *yes*, I'm gonna breed you, gonna marry you, gonna marry this fucking dream pussy- *fuck!*"

My mind blanked as that third wave barreled into me, and I blacked out to the thought of white dresses, babies and the terrifying realization that I was spiraling towards forever with someone I had barely known twenty-four hours ago.

And I wanted it.

Alicia

I watched as Honey grew limp beneath me, even as her walls kept milking me for every drop. I took advantage of her fainting spell to push her up into a mating press – I wasn't too far off to begin with- as my cock pressed a final shot of come against her cervix. *There, that should take.*

Despite my own growing tiredness, I pushed myself off the ground, hissing as my cock reluctantly left her cunt. Come dribbled from her still twitching lips, and I smirked in satisfaction. I stretched my sore muscles, relishing the burn, before gently scooping her up in my arms, carrying her to my king-sized bed, where she would stay for the next two day. I tucked her in, gazing fondly at her. Even in sleep, she carried that dick-dazed look from earlier. I pressed a lingering kiss to her lips, before heading back to tidy the evening's mess. I finished the last dregs of the wine as I moved about. My eyes caught on the dark patch of our mixed juices on the rug. *Maybe Honey did have a point*, I thought with another satisfied smirk. *Not that it would have changed the outcome.*

As soon as her throat swallowed my dick, I felt my last strands on control breaking, even as the pain of her teeth came moment later. I had just enough rational thought left to sense her panic over it and redirected her to my where my own weeping cunt desired some attention.

I thought her clear inexperience with women would serve to help me regain some of my senses. Instead, her pink tongue sucked the life from my clit, and I found my faint control slipping further away, and with her insistent mutterings about the *rug* instead of our pending fuck, I snapped completely. I wasn't exactly *proud* of the resulting coupling, but my gosh, how it satisfied every night I'd spent lost in my fantasies. I winced as I remembered just how loose my lips had gotten towards the end. I hadn't lied, but I saw her surprise even through the pleasured haze on her face.

I probably should've held those cards a little closer to my chest. She probably loved it in the moment, but marriage is not a discussion to have with someone you officially met yesterday.

Still, the thoughts, now that I'd spoken them out, filled my mind. While I'd never once tested my fertility, preferring condoms regardless of whether I was fucked or fucking, I was certain I had impregnated my little sexpot. The use of hormonal contraceptives had been made illegal decades ago, when the numbers first started their steady decline, therefore I knew Honey would not be on the pill or any other contraception, certainly not so close to her Change. I was months away from turning twenty-five, at the peak of my form. A child was almost a given certainty, and I strangely felt at peace with that.

Honey would make a phenomenal mother, and I daresay I was ready for a child of my own after spending so much time with Lily. She was such a sweet child and I was eager to see how our child would grow.

As for the marriage side of things- I really did believe we would do well together. Of course, now was too soon, and no one cared about whether children were born in or out of wedlock, so there was no rush or deadline. I firmly believed that, if our sex was any indication, we were very compatible indeed. All of that would follow in time.

 I grabbed our strewn clothing and brought them back to the room, putting them in the laundry basket. *If she needed clothes, she could wear something of mine,* I thought, before sliding into the bed besides her. She let out a soft whine, and I smiled softly, drawing her into my arms. Sleep came within moments.

I stirred awake to the sound of Honey moving about the living room, trying and failing to keep quiet as she fruitlessly searched for her clothes. I smiled into the pillow. *Come back to bed, Honey.*

I could tell the exact moment when she realised, she'd have to either wake me or make do with something of mine. I kept my eyes closed as she softly padded into the room, her footfalls cushioned by the tan carpet of the bedroom.

She paused somewhere at the foot of my bed, before making her way towards my head. I waited for her arm to reach out towards my shoulders. I quickly twisted around, grabbing her arm and waist, using her surprise and momentum to flip her over to the bed, rolling her under me, so my cock was nestled between her plump ass cheeks. She squeaked in surprise, and I laughed into her hair.

"Where did you think you were going, so bright and early?"

She huffed her response into the pillow.

"…I thought I should go home."

I laughed again.

"Home? No, baby, you're not going home for a little while yet."

I felt her tense in surprise. "But I thought-"

I cut her off, feeling my dick hardening between her plump flesh. "You thought what? You'd slip out like a thief, leaving me in this cold bed alone, even as your cunt still drips with my come?"

She gave another huff, but her hips started rocking beneath mine, making my length pass over that tight rosebud ring. *One day, I fill you up here too. Once I've gotten you nice and round with our baby, I can't waste any come before then.*

"I- I know what you said yesterday was just, in the moment. And- I'm practically already- there probably isn't-"

I felt my relaxed state quickly melt away into a familiar lustful haze as she spoke. *Was she denying me already?*

"Isn't a baby? Is that what you were going to say?" She her head down, even as her hips raised, letting my dick slide down to her opening, already wet and leaking.

I tutted in realization.

"Oh Honey. Is this your way of asking me to make sure it takes? You don't have to worry about that- I have no intention of letting you go anywhere this weekend." I let myself enter her in a slow press, gliding though effortlessly. I hissed at the tightness of her walls, feeling them twitch against me sporadically. *This* was home.

"As for the rest," I reached over for a pillow, sliding it beneath her for the perfect angle, hissing as I pressed against her cervix once more, my balls lightly batting against her clit. I took a moment to savor the sensation of her around me.

"I meant every word."

Her breath hitched. "…Really?"

I softly kissed her cheek. "Yes. I know it's too soon, but I like you, a lot. It doesn't have to be next week, it doesn't have to be next year, but yes. I very much see us together for the rest of our lives."

"Oh."

I snorted. *Yes, 'oh'.*

"Now, can I fuck you into the mattress? Or do you have any more questions?"

"Yes," she squeaked.

"Yes what?"

"…Yes please."

"Yes please, you have more questions?"

"No! Yes…please…"

I waited as she trailed off. I knew exactly what she wanted the first time, but I wanted to hear it come from her lips. When the silence dragged on, I stopped my light rocking, subconsciously done, and waited. She squirmed at my lack of movement, but I lightly swatted her ass, both cheeks at a time, and she clenched hard around me, raising her hips in response. I couldn't help but give her three harsh thrusts despite my intention to wait, her pussy just felt too good, my hips were on automatic. I forced myself to still, spanking her again for her naughtiness.

You are way too tempting like this, fuck.

"Yes please, *what?*"

"...Yes, please fuck me into the mattress."

I smirked.

"With pleasure."

Honey

I moaned as I slid into the hot bath Alica prepared for me. The scent of honey and vanilla was not lost on me, and I smiled softly. *You really were obsessed.* Every muscle ached, even those I didn't know *could* ache. My ass in particular was sore, a combination of the many spankings I didn't know I'd like, and being bent in a series of positions that really shouldn't have been possible. My yoga classes really paid off over the last two days, although with next to no rest in between, my muscles felt wringed out, so I insisted on stretching properly before bed last night.

Alicia surprisingly joined me, knowing most of the moves, displaying a range of flexibility on *her* part that made me a little envious, while simultaneously wondering how these moves could be applied in *other* situations. My mind was intrigued. My *vagina* on the other hand, was done. KO'd.

Deceased, and happier for it. Alicia's monster cock didn't spare me an inch, whether in length or girth-\still didn't know how she crammed it all inside, particularly in *during* 'downward facing dog'.

I hissed as the water caused my swollen lips to sting.

Soft but firm hands slid down my sides, shifting to lightly massage my lower back muscles. I smiled softly as the sound of water sloshing about filled the room, and Alicia's golden legs framed mine, her breasts pressed into my back as she lured me to rest in her arms.

"I did go hard on you," she started, a pang of regret in her voice. I quickly hushed her.

"I loved every second. Although…" I trailed off, wondering about my next thought. Alicia's fingers tightened minutely.

"Although?"

"When do I get to fuck *you?*" I threw back, turning my head to see her better. I laughed at the confused smile on her face.

"Honey, you *are* fucking me."

I shook my head slowly and made sure to look her in the eyes. I simply quirked up an eyebrow and I'd never seen a more satisfying sight than her glowing red as my meaning dawned on her.

"You-you'd *want* to do that?"

I smiled shyly. "Of course, why wouldn't I? It's only fair."

Alicia drew me close, snorting as she kissed me softly. "I guess so. I just didn't expect Little Miss Honey to be into that."

I frowned, turning in her arms. "I've *explored* things before. Sexually." I shot her a teasing look. "You're not the first woman I've been with, although-" I glanced at her cock, resting on her thigh. *That* is *new.*

Alicia grabbed my chin to redirect my attention. "*Really?*"

I scowled. I may not have been the sex goddess she was, but surely, I wasn't *that* bad?

She rushed to placate me.

"Not that you were- I'm just surprised, that's all. Honey, you're one of those women who seem – destined to be with a man." Her eyes turned wicked as she leered at me. "At least, until a sexy she-devil cast a spell on you with her dick." I pushed her away, laughing.

"That had been the plan, I guess. But I'm glad you ruined it. This is far better than any white picket dream." Even as I spoke, I marveled at the truth of my words. Yes, the idea of having children still very much lingered within me, but Alicia had already given me so much joy and pleasure in the last four days, sometimes without meaning to. I hated the thought of losing that easiness. Children could be adopted, although the process was longer and more difficult than ever. But who would I have to grow old with? To laugh and tease? I couldn't imagine anyone but her.

Alicia's eyes grew suspiciously shiny, and she coughed wetly, drawing me back against her chest in the cooling water. I let her compose herself as I grabbed her hands in mine, playing with her finger.

After a moment, Alicia spoke, her voice slightly raspy.

"So. Tell me about yourself, Honey Jane."

I fidgeted slightly. "There's nothing much to say." I wasn't lying. My family were painfully ordinary, and we weren't particularly close.

I could feel Alicia's confusion behind me at my deflection.

"Still, there must be something to tell. I spilled all my family trauma- tell me our children will have at least *one* set of grandparents."

I frowned at the reminder of Alicia's past. "Wait. Alicia, you said they caught you, in the *bathroom.* Did they-?"

"See *all* of me? Yes." My hands tightened around hers. *I had been surprised, but I was a potential lover, not adoptive parents with no concept of privacy and boundaries. I can only imagine what they did.*

"I can practically *hear* you thinking the worst. Don't worry, they didn't touch me."

The unsaid *much* range very loud in the ensuing pause.

"My mother was horrified; thought I was a cross-dressing boy. There was lots of shouting and grabbing, which is when they both discovered my vagina."

Alicia lay her head against mine. Her voice grew slightly distant, as if reliving the moment she was unwillingly outed. Still, she continued.

"After that, no more touching. At all. They also left me alone, which unnerved me. I think going from constant harassing to complete isolation threw me off, mentally. I started wearing revealing clothes, tight shorts that displayed my dick, with flowy tops that showcased my growing boobs, just so that they could give me some reaction, *anything*, even if only to tell me to get dressed properly. Then, my father got the bright idea to 'donate' me to medical researchers. The fertility of the humanity was lowering, here was this hybrid thing flaunting its abnormality, might as well kill two birds with one stone."

I gasped in horror at the thought of her on an examining table, as doctors poked and prodded at her.

"Surely he didn't-!"

"He didn't, but only because I caught on, and ran away. You see, he wanted compensation for his unique discovery, but the facility must've demanded proof of sorts. He came into my room when he thought I was sleeping, Mother too. She did the actual *handling*, and he took the pictures. The next day, I was gone. I didn't know exactly what the pictures were for, I suspected a porn magazine at the time, but I didn't want to wait and find out."

"How did you find out? About the medical researchers?"

"Ariana confronted them. I told her about them taking photos, and she flew over to get them, blackmail them, I don't exactly know the details, but she told me they confessed to it all, after realizing Ariana knew about me. I don't think they suspected her either, but I'm not sure."

"Did your brother know? Afterwards? I know you all are estranged from them now." I explained.

Alicia shook her head. "Ari told him they took photos of me naked, left it at that. He'd always wanted children, so I guess the thought of keeping in contact with them freaked him out enough to cut them off completely in solidarity."

I shuddered at the thought of despicable people like that anywhere near sweet Lily. Even without the knowledge of what Alicia was, their attitude towards the siblings was alarming to hear as a teacher.

Alicia bit my ear lightly, drawing me from my thoughts.

"Anyway, then I came out here after completing high school and college uneventfully, met my niece, fell for her teacher, a tempting little thing who, even after seeing me and hearing of all my past trauma, refused to tell me anything about her own past."

I squirmed in response. She had a point there. She shared so much of herself with me, why was I so reluctant to share my own past? I braced myself and searched for where to begin.

"Okay- so, I was born here, in Windermere. My parents were both teachers, lecturers at the University of Florida, my mother in social ethics, my father in economics."

I grimaced as I remembered all the lectures I was treated to growing up. "Even before the epidemic, my parents struggled to conceive. My brother and I were the result of their eleventh round of IVF."

"You both? You have a twin?" Alicia interjected. I could hear her surprise.

"Not really? I mean, in the technical sense, as in we both occupied her womb at the same time, but we're very much fraternal. His name is Harry. Well- Harrison, officially, but we've always called him Harry."

Honey and Harry Jane. That was us. Two individually fertilized eggs forced to cohabite the same womb for nine months, resulting in dizygotic 'twins'. Perhaps we were close in the womb, but as soon as we born, we were carted off in two separate directions. Even the way we were born was separate. I brushed past that, thinking of what else Alicia might like to know.

"I had a pretty typical childhood. Ballet, gymnastics, violin, flute, pink room, babies, teddies, barbie dolls, the whole nine yards."

Alicia laughed. "You were a real girly-girl, weren't you?" I shrugged lightly. *Yes, I was*.

"I think my parents felt that since they had one of each, and more siblings were highly unlikely, they may as well ensure we were perfect. Harry played sports and piano, guitar and video games, was in the math club and everything. Like I said, pretty boring."

Alicia hummed into my hair. "Your parents sound almost as anal as mine, albeit in a slightly healthier way. I bet you had doors. *Lots* of them."

"Yes, not that they were closed much. There was always someone to entertain, work colleagues to meet, dinner parties with other perfect children, who we were expected to take on a *tour* of the rooms." I rolled my eyes. "Not that we ever actually played. Everyone was so fixed into their roles that we *pretended* to. Held the babies, braided the doll's hair for the parents to see and coo over, but once they were gone, we'd just sit in silence."

Alicia froze for a second. "Shit, Honey. That sounds so-*sad*."

I laughed, turning to face her once more. "It really was. But again, harmless."

Alicia wore a slight scowl.

"I disagree. Baby, I hope you know that our kids aren't gonna be forced into *anything*. They're playing what they want to, with *who* they want to. None of that phony shit."

I laughed again. "Anyway, Harry is now a surgeon in pediatrics," to which Alicia gave a low whistle. Any sector where you worked with children was already highly perceived, but to actively save them? That carried *a lot* of weight. Which Harry never seemed to forget. "Oh yes, he's quite a bigshot in the city. He met his wife Rachel during his residency, a pediatric nurse, and they had a son three years ago, Jacoby Jane the second, after my father. I haven't seen him much beyond photos, but he was a very cute baby."

Harry and Rachel claimed the journey from Jacksonville was too arduous for them to make, and so I visited during Christmas when I could, although last year I felt too sick to travel, and settled for a card and presents sent via mail. My parents travelled often since their retirement, often spending weeks at a time with their successful son and beloved grandson.

"You don't see them much?"

"Not really. It's a two-hour journey, and even then, Harry and I were never that close to begin with."

Alicia gave me a pitiful look. "What about your parents?"

I shrugged slightly. "We're not that close either to be honest. They weren't the most affectionate growing up, and even though they still live here, they're always travelling for one thing or the other, so we don't see each other much. They do spend a lot of time with Jacoby though."

"I'll shower you and our kids with all the affection in the world."

I smiled into the kiss I pressed on her lips.

Over the past days, Alicia hadn't slowed down with the talk of babies and our future children. While I had been hopeful at first, reality fast caught up to me, and I realised I was months, if not *weeks* away from the Change. Alicia was twenty-four. There was still enough time for her to have children, whether by carrying them or fathering them, although I was certain the latter would not be with me. Still, a wistful thought crossed my mind.

Your children will be so blessed to have you as their mother.

Alicia

"Why are you smiling, *tita*?"

I glanced into my rearview mirror at my sweet niece.

"I'm not smiling." I was indeed smiling.

"I can see you," came her response.

"If I *were* smiling, it would be because I'm happy," I retorted.

"Are you happy then? Because you're smiling," Lily replied, her eyes shrewder than they ought to have been on a five-year-old. *You know, sometimes you really look like your mother.* I decided to stop teasing her.

"I am happy," I said with a large grin, and Lily nodded, satisfied. I focused on the road as I thought of my little sexpot, rushing through her morning routine to get to work on time. I was quite serious about her not going home till Monday, but I'd been generous and let her shower and borrow a few of my clothes before heading out, rather than do the walk of shame from the building.

The shower was of course shared, to conserve water, and to allow me to fuck her how I wanted against the tiled walls.

She left with a creampie to go with the vanilla cream latte I made her. *A little good luck for the day.*

"Why are you happy, *tita*?"

I hummed. "Because I had a very good breakfast." Her cunt had tasted of the cinnamon bath scents we'd used last night, with vague hints of the strawberry lotion I'd slathered her in, and I licked it all up before fucking her against the wall. Delicious.

But I couldn't tell the five-year-old that thinking about her teacher's pussy made me very happy, so I kept it vague.

"I had a cinnamon roll with strawberry milk."

Of course she did.

"Mama made it because Jessica wasn't home. Mama was really angry, she said Jessica was in a fire. I hope she's okay," Lily continued innocently, oblivious to the havoc she'd caused.

Jessica had been fired. When? I wondered if Emilia had found out about her trysts with Ariana. Neither had made any effort to hide it, and the last time I'd see her,

Jessica had been a right mess, freshly fucked and barely present. It was a wonder she'd made it this long, really. I really hoped she wasn't pregnant, that would over complicate things. I also wondered if Ariana was aware, although I highly suspected so. There wasn't much she didn't know.

That did explain the seven am text from Enri requesting I drop my niece off to school. Not that I minded much, it gave me another reason to see my honeypot. Matter of fact, I volunteered for the next three weeks.

"It's a pity about Jessica, sweetheart, I know you liked her."

"It's okay. Mamma said I can have a manny now. That's a boy nanny."

I smirked to myself. If Emilia thought that would stop Ariana from getting her dick, or any other part of her wet, for that matter, she was sorely mistaken.

"Mm, okay sweetie, sounds fun- let's get you to class."

I pulled up into the drop off bay, quickly hopping out so I could get the door for her. We marched to the open school gates, Lily skipping besides me, waving to her many friends, eagerly chattering on about her best friends, and all the things they were going to talk about. I tried to pay attention, but I quickly lost interest, as my eyes rested on a gorgeous pair of blue eyes, twinkling at me from across the hall. I winked, and she smiled back at me, making her way across to us, waving at parents and children alike as they made their way into the classroom. A few stares were curiously tossed our way.

That's right, we get a personal escort, because we're very important people.

"Hi Lily," Honey started, crouching down to talk to the five-year-old, giving me time to check out her outfit for the day. *Wait a minute, is that…?*

The little minx wore my favourite gym shirt, loosely disguised as professional wear with the dress slacks and knitted cardigan she wore over it.

Marking your territory, baby? I like it.

"- And how are you today, Miss Padrilla?"

I looked up to find her smirking at me. *Damn minx knew what she was doing.*

"Pretty good, Miss Honey. I got a lot of stretching and exercise done this weekend."

She pinkened slightly, and I was happy to get a rise out of her. But Lily stole the show entirely.

"*Tita* had a really good breakfast this morning."

I guffawed as Honey's pink turned crimson, and she sent me a withering look as she whisked Lily into class. Other parents stared at me a bit funny, but I ignored them as I spotted her hiding a smile as she closed the kindergarten door.

Too easy.

I sent her a quick test as I went back to my car, before making my way to *Let Loose,* as usual. Marcie was already there, as usual, loading the protein machines as I stepped in. The green and black design cast the room in early morning shadows, and I was able to creep up on Marcie, long enough to hear her mutterings, unmuffled as they were by the music system's lack of base.

"- stupid, arrogant, *insufferably hot-*"

"One of those three is not the same," I snarked, making my way to the side of the machine, where Marcie had tucked herself. Baleful eyes met mine.

"He. Is. All. *Three.*" She returned to the machine, where I could now see she had been messing with the wires and parts at the back of the display panel. Whenever there was a problem she couldn't fix, Marcella turned to two things- alcohol and tinkering with electronics.

Judging by the mess of wiring I was peering at, evidently this business partner was a *huge* problem, one that had made itself at home in her beloved gym.

Marcie was hunched over a circuit panel, picking at the wires like it owed her money.

"So," I said cautiously. "You look... *happy*. What happened?"

She didn't even look up. "That potential business partner I told you about? The one who came by yesterday? For whom I bought *air fresheners?* Absolute asshole."

I leaned against the vending machine, an eyebrow quirked. "What'd he do?"

Marcie finally focused on me, eyes blazing. "What *didn't* he do? He had some *choice* things to say about every last detail. The scuff marks on the floor. The slightly worn boxing ring ropes. The paint color. The lighting. The *airflow*, for fuck's sake. He walked in and immediately started tearing the place apart- at *four am-* and then he moved on to me."

I blinked. "Wait. He found something wrong with you? You're a gorgeous, hard-working, intelligent babe who built everything from the bottom up, *quite literally* at times—"

It's true. When I joined, it was a warehouse with a few gym mats on the floor and a hanging punching bag I *strongly* suspected she made herself from a laundry bag and sand from the sea. Why did I think that? Because she had me make the next *three*.

Marcie cut me off with a bitter laugh. "He thought I was a homeless person sneaking in to take advantage of the gym's, and I quote, 'abysmal security system.'"

I couldn't help laughing at that. It wasn't awful but it certainly needed improvements. It was a keypad and two deadbolts- holding shut a sliding warehouse door, which was often left open during the day. It wasn't as though there were many people to keep *out* per say, but still- it *would* be abysmal to a big-wig city guy.

Still- he thought she was *homeless?* "Why?!" I wheezed out.

"I'd just come out of the showers," she said, throwing her hands up. "Hair in a mask, face covered in a sheet mask. He sees me, freezes, and then berates me for trespassing. I manage to say that I work here, and then he switches gears and accuses me of misusing company property."

I was doubled over now, but she wasn't done.

"Then," she continued, "he proceeds to rip into everything he doesn't like about the gym. Every corner, every piece of equipment. And he wraps it all up by saying he's looking forward to teaching 'Marcel'—" she made air quotes "—a thing or two about order and running a business."

I straightened, still grinning, but that faded slightly when I noticed how tightly she was gripping her soldering iron. "Why is this getting to you so much? You haven't signed anything. Everyone in town knows how hard you work. A couple more donations and you'll get that en suite. You don't *need* this guy."

She stared at me for a long beat, jaw tight. Then she leaned forward and hissed, "I don't need him, no. *But I want him.*"

I froze. "You—what?"

She threw herself back into the vending machine circuitry, scoffing as she identified the wire that has causing her so much grief, it seemed. "Yeah. Have fun trying to figure that one out. Weeks of *nothing* from my *dick,*" she lowers her voice as one of the local shop boys walk past on their way to the ellipticals. "A sweet girl with a great rack wrestling with me- nothing. A hot dude with hench arms flirting with me- nothing. A giant scarred asshole with a snobby attitude and a limp? *Hard as titanium.* It took three orgasms just to calm it down, and I had to imagine him yelling at me for it to work. *What is that?!*" she exclaims hotly. I'm knocked damn near speechless. So *this* is what did it for her? This Change business for us really was a mess. Ariana can't help but fuck anything that moves, Marcie now had a Pavalovian response to humiliation it seemed- I feared my own response.

I felt my phone buzz and quickly checked my messages. Hopefully, Honey and I were in a much better place, settles with kids by the time I had to concern myself with whatever madness was overtaking my friend and sister.

And that would start with her response. My jaw dropped slightly, and Marcie caught sight. She rolled her eyes.

"*Please* tell me you and Miss Yoga Pants are a thing. Let my bad luck be the result of someone's good fortune."

I had no idea what to say, so I just stood there, my brain short-circuiting between lust, disbelief, and the urge to laugh again.

- Breakfast was indeed delicious, most important meal of the day. ;D
- I'd like to make sure I never miss it- want to go out for dinner tonight? Maybe catch a film after?

You're right, a nutritious breakfast is very important-

I was very naughty and had only had a pie ;) -
How about we catch that movie at your place? - That way you can make sure I swallow all of my protein shake -

And I'll make sure you get your honey. -

This woman will be the end of me.

"You'd better get ready for a world of misfortune, Marcie. My luck is far from running out."

Honey

Hi baby ;o –

*I'll be a little late to dinner tonight, Marcie's –
overwhelmed with all the renovations*

Keep it warm, I'll make it up to you ;D–

I couldn't fight the grin taking over my face as I read
Alicia's words, turning my phone back over to pay
attention to the kids as they quietly worked on their
shapes. I stood and began my tour of the room, pausing
occasionally to help the children focus on their task,
answering questions and complimenting their attempts.

All the while my thoughts were of *her*.

The past three months had been a dream; every morning, I woke with our limbs twined together in a mess of arms and legs. Unravelling them led to morning shenanigans that never failed to make me blush- this morning, I had taken charge, in anticipation of the dinner I had planned for tonight. I suckled on her cherry bud and helped myself to her tight cunt as she slept, my fingers drilling her violently, till she jolted, awakened by the force of her orgasm.

She proceeded to test out how many orgasms she could give during our admittedly short fifteen-minute window. My legs still twitched sporadically through the day.

"Miss Janey, please can I have some help?" Lily's voice wafted up from the general murmurings of the class.

"Of course you can," I said, as I made my way over to her. I wondered if my growing favoritism was obvious to the others. I hoped not, but I couldn't deny that I was favoring her. Even before Alicia came into my life, I felt a connection to young Lily, but now, I felt it was as though we were family, and I rarely said no to her. Good thing she was such a sweet child, goodness knows where what she'd have gotten away with otherwise.

"I don't know what these shapes are," she said, the frustration clear in her. I glanced at her work, realizing it was the 3D shapes that were tripping her up. I quickly went through the list with her again, and she nodded, making corrections before I moved on.

There was a knock at the door, and I glanced up, frowning slightly when I saw Susan there.

If the three months past had been bliss, Susan had been a thorn in my side. Since the discussion about the upcoming trip, set for the last day of school, Susan and a few of her cronies hadn't failed to bring it up almost every chance they could. I sidled away as often as I could, but they had caught me a few times, each discussion more grating than the last. I had even taken to eating at the back of my classroom, in quick bites, sometimes not even finishing my meal, so eager was I to stay busy and out of the way.

I could feel my resolve weakening, despite Alicia's many encouragements. *Maybe they really need me.*

I left Lily's side and directed Susan to the cramped supply closet at the back of my room, sitting on the table. Susan stood awkwardly opposite me, scanning my face with an inscrutable expression. No matter, I knew what this was about the moment Susan appeared at my classroom door.

Her smile was too tight, her eyes too fixed.

The air inside was stifling—thick with the smell of disinfectant spray- always kept on hand with so many young stick fingers and seasonal colds- and the smell of new plastics and old cardboard. I wrinkled my nose at the surprising strong smell, and leaned against the small shelves, keeping my mouth shut. I didn't need to prompt her; I knew she'd get to it. *And since you interrupted my class, you can take the lead here.*

It took a while, but eventually sensing I had no intentions of speaking, Susan broke the silence.

"I need you to reconsider the trip," she said at last, folding her arms tightly.

I could feel the heat prickling at my skin as she started. *That's it? No please, no 'I'm sorry for being a pushy hag, but I'm old and a bitch- please forgive me and consider the children you love being stuck with me.'*

"I know you've led the last three trips," she continued, "and even stepped in for other teachers. That's exactly why you'd be perfect. It's the last one before the holidays—you'll have time to rest after. It's just a waste to have such an experienced and capable teacher doing nothing."

You have six more years of experience on me. than

I drew in a breath, ready to speak, but she cut me off.

"And before you say no again, most of the planning's already done. Me, Rachel, Mr. Patel—we've sorted it."

There was something in her tone—just a faint edge—that made it sound like she thought I was being lazy. As if my reluctance had nothing to do with the truth: that every trip meant carrying the weight of keeping a group of tiny, unpredictable children safe in a world full of hazards. Every headcount was a silent prayer. With the birth rate falling, each child felt even more precious, and the responsibility pressed heavily on my shoulders. *How dare she.*

"It's not about the planning," I said quietly, trying to reign in my temper, the heat of June seemingly made its way into the tiny room, causing my skin to prickle and my head to grow faint. *I can't keep doing this for the next week.*

"It's the responsibility. They're so young, and if anything happened—"

"Nothing will happen," she interrupted sharply. "We've covered every detail. You just have to show up."

"I've already showed up! Several times, as you pointed out. I just want -" The room seemed to shrink around me. My chest tightened. I hadn't had a proper lunch in days, always cutting it short or rushing to find something else to do so I wouldn't be cornered like this. And now here I was, cornered anyway, the lack of food and stress getting to me. And Susan showed no signs of slowing down.

"What you *want* isn't of importance here, ~~Susan.~~ Jane. This is about what would be *best,* and-"

"I really need to get back to my class," I murmured hotly, stepping toward the door, towards my students and the open windows.

"Jane, wait—"

"*My name isn't Jane!*"

I whirled as her hand caught my arm. The movement threw me off balance, and my elbow clipped the edge of a stack of whiteboard boxes. They tumbled, causing other boxes to fall from the higher shelves, one catching me square on the temple.

The world went white.

Somewhere far away, I heard my students shouting, their voices high and panicked. Sirens followed, rising and falling like waves. Then nothing.

When I next opened my eyes blearily, the ceiling above me was a flat, sterile white. Fluorescent lights buzzed softly, and I flinched at the brightness of it all. I was lying on a paper-covered bed, a nurse checking my vitals with calm efficiency.

"Good afternoon, Miss Jane. Do take your time, and please don't get up just yet. Give your stomach time to settle," she cooed down at me, pressing at my damp brow with a cool cloth.

I blinked about me, confused. It took a moment for the memories to return—the closet, the heat, the box. The trip. Susan.

I hadn't given her an answer. But maybe my body had already given one for me.

"Did I faint? Oh gosh, the children! They must've seen me- they'll be so worried!" I jolted up in horror, thinking of all their little faces, confused and concerned.

"There, there now," the nurse shushed me gently, easing me back down, fluffing my pillow as she did. "That isn't for you to worry about anymore. The doctor will be in shortly, and she'll take you through it all."

My confusion must've showed on my face. The nurse beamed down at me. She looked around before quickly squeezing my hand and pressing a kiss against my cheek. "Congratulations!" she whispered, before darting out.

I froze in shock. *What on earth...?*

The nurse unnerved me, and I hesitated in getting up, despite the uncomfortable angle I was in. Instead, I focused on the room around me, wincing when I realised it was a private suite. *My insurance will not cover this.*

A gentle came at the door, and I turned, watching as a tall South Asian woman came in, her white coat swinging gently around wide hips. Her hair was blue, to my surprise, a deep navy blue, with teal highlights beneath, visible as she turned to check my vitals. Her eyes, when they turned on me, were a warm honey brown, complimenting her soft burgundy lips as she smiled at me.

"Hello Miss Jane. I'm Doctor Kudira, and I've got some very exciting news for you today," she said gently.

"Hi, please, call me Honey." I peered towards her chart, wondering what she found. I perked up suddenly. *Maybe the Change is further away than I thought! Maybe I was ovulating, or something all this time!*

"Alright then, Honey. Now you've had a rough knock to the head, which concerned us as judging from what the paramedics said, the boxes that actually fell on you weren't heavy enough to cause a concussion, however you were passed out for a while. So, we took some mandatory blood tests and were quite alarmed when we discovered your condition. A fall could really have caused injuries, and to be honest, your job is quite stressful to begin with, as shown by your elevated levels."

complications

I deflated as she spoke. "Yes, I'm aware. I'd been on the verge for a while, but I guess it's truly upon me now," I said. *The Change really is upon me, now. Fuck Susan, she can go on the trip herself.*

Dr. Kudira frowned. "You knew about your condition? But kept working?"

"It didn't affect me much, beyond headaches and occasional flashes. Although I have been feeling dizzy lately, but I thought that was from the lack of food."

Her face grew alarmed. "You've been experiencing dizziness and lack of nourishment? For how long?"

I squinted at the ceiling, trying to recall just when I'd started noticing my symptoms.

"Last September or so? My period became really irregular around December, I think I've skipped it a couple of times since then."

Her brows drew together. "Miss Honey, you're only about three months along, and your body shows no signs of previous miscarriages. However, your medical history alarms me, and so I'd like us to take a few more tests…" Her voice trailed off as she took in my obvious surprise. "Honey- you are aware that you are indeed pregnant?"

My mind blanked. "But- my partner and I, it wasn't- she- wait,"

Dr. Kudira's watched me patiently. "Are you and your partner sexually active? Or rather, I believe you mentioned her pronouns were feminine, had you not been looking into sperm donations, or fertility treatments?"

"No, I thought I was entering the Change, we never used protection-" I briefly remembered not to mention Alicia's special tool. But wait- she could be transgender. It's not like they do physical checks on the father, so Dr. Kudira wouldn't know Alicia was a futanari.

Dr. Kudira's face cleared slightly. "Ah, I see. Honey, not to be indelicate, but does you partner have an intact male appendage? Because even with the hormonal therapy, their testicles would still continue sperm production."

I snorted. *As if Alicia ever halted sperm production. She insisted on pumping me so often, her balls had no choice* but *to produce more.*

"I can tell this is a surprise to you. If you want, you can come back with your partner for the first ultrasound, and I can answer any queries then."

I nodded absently; my brain still hung up on that word. *Pregnant. I was pregnant!*

My breath hitched as tears filled my eyes. I placed trembling hands on my stomach.

"Are you-are you *sure?*" I couldn't help asking once more. Dr. Kudira placed a hand over mine.

"Honey, I'm more positive than your blood test- in six months, you're having a baby."

Alicia

I frowned down at my phone.

Still no response from Honey.

I put my phone away, focusing on the floor polish Marcie and I were applying. It made no sense to me, but Marcie had decided to proceed with the investor, if only for the orgasms, I assumed. Technically his ideas weren't *wrong*, merely uptight, so I couldn't begrudge the gradual changes being made. Still, it felt like a waste of money to me, but at least it was from his own pockets.

I glanced across at Marcie, who stood across the hall texting furiously, her long hair swept up in a messy bun. She had grease on her face and clothes, but she paid it no mind. I watched as she let out a growl, took a selfie of herself giving the middle finger, making sure to have the wet floor in the background, sending it with a string of curses. I couldn't contain my laughter.

"Marcie, this flirting thing you guys have going on, when will it end?"

She shot me a heated glare. "Oh, I'm sorry, *how long did you and Miss Yoga Pants dance around each other?*"

I laughed again. In the past couple of months, Honey and Marcie had been reintroduced, although Marcie insisted on the nickname staying. The two got along spectacularly, although that first night at the bar, when Honey found out we used to fuck, there had been a glorious display of possessiveness I didn't even know she was capable of.

Honey had all but given me a lap dance at the bar, before hissing in Marcie's face, "I can fuck her better than you." Ignoring Marcie's amused snorts, Honey had dragged me home and proceeded to do just that, with a cute purple strap-on ensemble that had fast become a bedroom favourite, leaving our drinks untouched with a faintly amused and stressed-out Marcie.

I'm certain they didn't go to waste.

A phone chime jolted me from my thoughts, and I rushed to draw my phone out, only for it to belong to Marcie's cell. She stared at her phone in disbelief, before flashing the screen around to me.

Even from across the room, I could make out perfectly chiseled abs, a deliciously dark happy trail leading down towards black sweatpants. The torso was littered in scars and tattoos, most too far away for me to make out. But what was very clearly visible, was the hastily scrawled note, saying YOU MISSED A SPOT.

taped to his chest,

The man was clearly in the middle of a workout, but decided antagonizing Marcie would be a much better source of endorphins. I let out a low whistle. Even though I was beyond thrilled with my little sexpot, even I could admire the work of art that was this mysterious man's torso.

Marcie shook the phone, as if she could shake the man. "Insufferable, but so hot! Why?!"

She didn't seem to realize her sparring shorts were sporting the mild tent of a chubbing dick, and I shook my head.

"You might wanna go take care of that," I said, nodding down towards her cock. Marcie groaned.

"I shouldn't reward it," she said, but even I heard the longing she couldn't quite hide.

I waved her off. "Go ahead, make use of that new en suite jacuzzi bath. I have." I shot her a leering smirk as my meaning dawned on her. "YOU-EW!" she screeched, and I cackled as she stormed off towards her studio, murmuring about disinfecting surfaces. She seemed to think I couldn't see her hand darting down to her probably straining dick, even as her other fingers caressed the phone screen.

You ain't cleaning nothing but your pipes.

Another chime came through, followed by a second. It was Honey, followed by Emilia. I opened Honey's first.

> *Hi Alicia, could you come home as soon as – possible? I've got some news.*

I frowned, a weird sensation in the pit of my stomach. *Everything was going well, at least, I thought it was. Did something happen at work?*

I checked the time- just after lunch. Too late to call her, I started tapping out a reply, when Emilia's text caught my eye.

> *Your sister is avoiding me. Your brother isn't ever in the mood. I know you've been feeling ___ stressed. Let's talk about it.*
>
> *I need to unwind. –*

I blinked at the screen. This woman was persistent. I swiped the message away, intending to respond to Honey, when the sound of heels filled the hall.

The sliding doors had been left open to allow the polish to circulate, but it seemed Marcie's investor was right- it was a shit fucking security system.

I sighed as Emilia turned the corner, all heels, legs and a suspicious trench coat in the middle of June. Her face was slightly pinched, faint lines marring her beauty.

"Why have you all been ignoring me?"

I quirked a brow. "I just saw your text."

She brushed me off. "Before that. Ariana is MIA after fucking my nanny stupid, despite her knowing Lily's birthday is around the corner in July. Enri is pulling all sorts of hours at work as if I haven't already given him the best job security in the world. And *you*," She levels a perfectly manicured nail at my chest, her steps closing the few metres I tried to keep between us.

"I'm not avoiding anyone; I'm helping with Lily after your impromptu sacking of the help." I interjected.

"Jessica needed to go, and you know it. I should've known Ariana would go after her, she never could resist a ripe womb." I scrunched up my nose in disgust. She wasn't wrong, but still. That was my sister.

"You-" Emilia halted, our chests almost pressing into each other. "You've been *so* attentive, I can hardly account for it. Why, it's almost like you've been searching for an outlet, a way to *unwind*." Her voice took on a crooning tone, and alarm bells started ringing in my head.

Her hands reached out to me, and I batted them away softly. *Time to nip this firmly in the bud.*

"Look, Emilia, I'm not searching for *anything*, I'm happy, I'm content- I'm just here for Lily." I said, pushing past her.

"Well maybe I can give you your own child, like I did your sister. How much more attentive would you be with a child of your own? Not a niece, but your own baby, to love and raise how you'd like?"

My eyebrows jumped at her words. *I guess subtlety was all out the window now.*

I turned to reject her but was surprised by the sight of her open coat, sliding to the floor, revealing her nude frame. Pregnancy had been kind to her, her model frame retained its toned muscles, with only her wider soft hips and slight silvery marks to hint at Lily's birth. Still, gorgeous or no, she was not for me. I backed away.

"Emilia-" but before I could finish, she pounced on me, knocking us to the sticky ground. I swore as polish got in my hair and tried to pry her off. But Emilia was no novice to wrestling, she took several Krav Maga lessons a week, and it paid off. She clung to me like a barnacle, pressing her tits into my face as her legs wrapped around my waist. I rolled her over into the ground, attempting to throw her off by the stickiness of the ground but before I could do so, a sharp gasp filled the room.

My head shot up and I swore forcefully.

Honey stood there, a box of my favourite pastries in hand, although the box now slipped from her hands into the floor polish.

My heart began to pound, and I made use of Emilia's surprise to finally pry her off. That only drew Honey's attention to Emilia's nudity, and her eyes filled with tears.

"Honey, it's not what it looks like-"

"Honey? Lily's teacher?" Emilia at least had the decency to blush.

Honey paid her no mind, instead gazing into my eyes with a dawning horror.

"You- your - *Lily*."

I frowned at the nonsensical thought. What did Lily have to do with...?

Wait. No!

"No- no- no, I'm not- that's wrong, she's my *niece*, Honey, I would never-"

Honey turned and ran out before I could finish my scattered thoughts, and I chased after her without a second thought. I heard Marcie step out from her room, no doubt in her robe wondering about the noise. I heard her shock at seeing Emilia rolling around in her polish, but I ignored them, focusing on getting to Honey as soon as possible.

Fuck, fuck, FUCK.

"Honey, wait! Nothing happened! I swear! It isn't-"

Honey darted back into her car, pulling away as I ran after her, leaving me standing in the parking lot, my heart breaking with every increasing space between us. I scrambled for my phone, calling Honey, but her voicemail greeted me repeatedly. Hand's trembling, I called my sister, only one thought running through my mind:

Honey

It's not what it looks like. It wasn't what it looked like.
She definitely wasn't rolling on top of Lily's naked
mother. Lily definitely wasn't her –

I abruptly cut my thoughts off. I wasn't prepared to face them. I liked to think I was a rational person, but there was too much to focus on, and I had already received my dose of life-changing news for the day.

I had sent Alicia a text as I left the doctor's office, but I changed my mind as I headed home, wanting to surprise her straight away. Instead, it seemed I was the one being surprised.

My phone rang again, and I reached out with a fumbling hand, switching off the ringer and tossing it in the back seat. I didn't want to hear any placations just yet, even if it *was* just a misunderstanding. I couldn't shake the sight of Lily's features spread across both of their faces. I knew Lily and Alicia bore some resemblance to each other, but I thought it was just as aunt and niece but seeing her with Lily's mother only highlighted where the two came together.

I realised I had started absentmindedly heading home, but I quickly pulled over on the bridge before I made the turn to my house. I pressed my head back against the headrest, trying to I think of where I could go. I suspected Alicia would be look for me there, and I wasn't up to it yet. Maybe there was nothing there, but even the possibility of there having *been* something once upon a time, threw me off mentally.

A beep came from behind me, and I jumped, relaxing when I saw it was only a delivery truck. I waved in apology, and started driving, making sure to turn away from my street. Instead, I took a side road towards an address I hadn't been to in ages. I put the radio on to pass the time, trying to pin the unease in my stomach on my newly discovered state, instead of dread towards the coming visit.

I pulled up to the quaint four-bedroom home, the hedges perfectly trimmed, the lawn a perfect shade of green, even in the heat of the summer sun. A gleaming hatchback sat in the driveway, beside a sleek sportscar. I squeezed into the last spot of the three-car driveway, exhaling slowly as I made sure not to bump into the expensive car.

The lights were all on inside, and faint music could be heard, making my stomach drop further. *Great. Another dinner party.*

I left my jacket in the car, but brought my purse with me, hoping to hide the fact that I came uninvited, and very much emptyhanded.

I gently raised the heavy door knocker, tapping it three times lightly. Even with the music, I knew it would be audible from experience.

Just as I was about to chicken out, the door swung open, revealing my mother's perfectly coiffed hair, matching her pearl and tartan suit ensemble. Her dazzling smile dropped slightly when she saw me, and I fought a wince. *Yes, why should you be excited to see your daughter, who you haven't called or visited in months, despite living in the same town.*

"Hi mom," I started, leaning down to give her a kiss in greeting, as was custom. Her jaw was tense, and I pulled away quickly.

"Honey. What a surprise, I didn't realize you were coming today." She said, false sincerity dripping from her strained smile. "Well, don't just stand there, come in, you're messing up the temperature in the house." She turned and headed back down the long corridor, making sure to shut a few doors along the way. I rolled my eyes. *Embarrassed your friends will see your daughter looking so scruffy?* I glanced down at my simple summer dress and brown loafers. *Very scruffy indeed.*

"How is work? I hear you're very good with the younger children. Winnie Mertl told me her grandson speaks very highly of you."

I smiled, thinking of the adorable black boy who always brought me flowers on a Monday, because his pops told him to always bring ladies flowers. Sure, they were usually ripped up daisies from the school field, but the gesture was really sweet.

"It's going pretty great, this year has been the best. And Artie is a very lovely and gifted child, Winnie should be very proud of him."

"Indeed, she is. Make sure to stay with the kindergarten next year, it is *such* an important slot, you were very lucky to land it this time."

Sure, lucky. It's not like I spent two years completing a master's degree to specialize in working with younger children.

Mom led me into the kitchen, ducking down to pull out a vase, only to freeze when she noticed my hands, empty but for the purse I held. "Oh. I'm sorry, that was instinctual. Guests usually bring flowers. Or wine. But I guess nothing will do nicely for your parents."

I couldn't hide my wince as my mother put the vase down by the island sink, leaving it there as if to remind me and anyone else of my shame. I noticed the other two bouquets and tried to change the subject.

"I recognized Mr Randall's car in the driveway." Tim Randall was the Dean of the university where my parents once taught. They retired with the birth of their grandson a couple of years ago, so I was mildly surprised to see his car here.

"Yes, he and Peggy wanted to come by and see- well, he's offered your dad another lecturing slot at the Symposium next month, so we invited them to dinner as a thank you."

I nodded absentmindedly. "I didn't recognize the other-"

"Mom, what's taking so long, the baby's getting restless?"

Harry's voice echoed through the corridor, and I jumped in shock. *So you* can *make it here?*

Harry looked upset to see me, which confused me further.

"Hi- "

"What are *you* doing here?" He swiveled to face Mom, anger in his tone. "Mom, why is she here? Rachel specifically requested you and dad not tell her."

My mouth dropped in surprise.

He turned back to me, his jaw tight, his eyes hard.

"I can't believe you've shown up here," he said, his voice low but sharp. "After last year? After everything?"

"What are you talking about?"

"You ignored Rachel through her entire pregnancy," he shot back. "It was a tough one, Honey. And then—" he gave a short, bitter laugh— "you send a Christmas card without even congratulating us on the birth of our son. No gift. Nothing. Do you have any idea how that felt?"

I was completely floored by his revelation. *Rachel was pregnant? A second son? What is happening today?*

"Harry, I didn't know. I had no idea she was pregnant, let alone that you'd had another baby."

He shook his head, lips curling in disbelief. "Don't lie to me. You expect me to believe you just… missed it? The biggest news in the family and you knew nothing?"

"Yes!" My voice rose before I could stop it. "Because no one told me! You didn't call, you didn't text, you didn't say a word. Mom-"

"I told Mom and Dad we were cutting contact with you," he said flatly. "I thought they'd make that clear."

I turned to look at Mom, who was stood by the edge of the counter, hands folded in front of her, watching us like she was waiting for the storm to pass. "You knew?" My voice cracked. "You, Dad- you knew, and you didn't say *anything*?"

She sighed, as if I'd asked her to explain something tedious. "Honey, you barely interact with any of us these days. There didn't seem much point in telling you."

The words hit harder than I expected. I stared at her, trying to process the casual cruelty in them.

I swallowed, forcing my voice to steady. "Can I at least meet my nephew?"

Harry glanced at the clock. "It's getting late. Rachel will be putting the kids to bed soon."

And just like that, he turned and walked out. I heard the door to the next room open, then Rachel's startled voice: "What happened?"

"I think we should go," she said after a moment, her voice carrying back to us.

From the kitchen, Dad's voice cut in, calm but firm. "No Rachel don't be silly. You and the kids will stay. Honey will leave, I don't know why she came in the first place, without a word to either of us."

The room felt suddenly smaller; the air heavier. I stood there for a moment, my hands cold and clammy as I tried not to faint again.

I still couldn't believe it.

"Mom, I've reached out to you guys, I send texts, I call when I can- there's a lot going on with work, but- even so. How could you not tell me?"

"In truth sweetheart, we thought we were doing you a favor. Already at work, you're surrounded by children, and you were so distant with Jacoby, your father and I though the news of Rachel's second baby would be too much. I know you're near *the Change*." She whispered the last part as if it were a curse I were about to inflict on innocent strangers. *Maybe she thought it was.*

Rachel was a year below me, perhaps they thought I'd somehow inflict the Change on her early. I blinked back the hot tears in my eyes, as I realised just how little my family really valued me. I had initially thought to announce my pregnancy, but how could I say anything now?

I wiped away the trickling tears.

"What's his name?" I asked, my voice small.

My mother beamed. "Rory. I picked it out, isn't it lovely?"

I didn't bother replying, heading for the living room, where I could hear voices muttering.

The room fell silent as I appeared. I took in Jacoby's toothy grin, and baby Rory's adorably plump cheeks, Rachel's distraught face, Harry's rage, and my father's displeased expression. I faintly noticed the horrified Randalls, no doubt told of my burning jealousy and spitefulness.

I took a deep breath, ready to plead my case, but my mother's hurried steps made me reconsider it all. *Why should I prove my innocence? My parents are right there, not speaking up for the lies they created. Harry immediately believed the worst about me, and Rachel-*

I turned to face her, and she flinched. I sighed.

- Rachel thinks I'm a jealous bitch. Never mind.

"The boys are adorable. Congratulations. I won't be able to travel up this Christmas either, but my door is always open." I turned to my parents, my mom having sidled up besides my dad, who hovered over his grandsons protectively. "Don't expect any calls from me."

With that I walked out of my childhood home, probably for the last time. I froze on the steps, seeing the tall, sharply dressed figure smoking on the hood of my car. For a I thought it was Alicia, but as I drew nearer, I noted the differences- cropped hair that I mistook for a ponytail, a sharper jaw and lips that- while soft- were pressed in a harder line than I'd ever seen on Alicia. The figure hopped down and put out their cigarette, grinding it into the ground before raising their head to meet my eyes. I gasped.

They were a *perfect* match to Lily's. Not in the way Alicia's were, no these could have been cut and pasted from child to adult- and vice versa.

This was-

"Ariana Padrilla. I'd say it's nice to meet you, but my sister is currently a mess, so I'd be lying if I did. That being said," Ariana peered at my tear slicked face, and her eyes flickered back towards the house. "You seem to be having a similarly shit time, so I'll ease off. Come," she held out for my key. "You're in no condition to drive."

I hesitated slightly. It's not that I didn't trust her, but the day had been full of surprises, I didn't think I could handle another. *The doctor said stress is bad for the baby.*

"Honey? Who is that? What's going on?"

My mother's false concern sent my heart pounding, and I dropped the keys in her hand with no further questions. We clambered in, Ariana swearing lightly as she adjusted the seat, before quickly taking off. I quietly marveled at her driving skills.

"So," she started. "I would ask what happened, but having estranged myself from my parents, I recognize the signs. Although I hated mine by the end, but I can tell from the hurt in your eyes, you still love them."

More tears eked out, and I hid a shuddering gasp in my hands. "They didn't tell me my brother and his wife were expecting. Then, they made them think I knew but was so jealous and spiteful that I ignored her through it all, and *worse*-"

"It gets *worse*?" Ariana muttered.

"When I was sick to my stomach last Christmas, she gave birth, and all I sent was a $75 dollar gift card, a diffuser and a remote-controlled car for the *one* nephew I knew of."

"Well. Shit."

I snorted. "Yep. Shit"

We drove in silence for a bit, before I realised she was taking me home.

"How did you know...?"

"I know everything about you, Honey Jane. Well, almost everything. Didn't know about the shit parents, but yeah. Everything. I even knew about your Rory. He was born via caesarean. There were complications, and they had to perform a partial hysterectomy. That's probably what made it seem so much worse. *Truly* shit parents."

I blinked silently. I would reach out to Rachel again. That must've been terrifying.

"I also know that you mistook whatever you think you saw this afternoon."

I flinched. *I wasn't ready for that-*

"I know it probably looked bad but trust me when I saw Alicia is head over sneakers for you." She shot me a smirk. "I never could get her to wear heels."

I laughed, feeling the weight of today ease from my chest.

"She hasn't even looked at another woman since she first saw you, or heck, your ass. And in truth, she probably never will. She's very all or nothing. And she's all in with you."

I could barely allow myself to believe in what I was hearing.

"I heard Lily's mother-"

"Emilia is beyond delusional at this point. It's my fault, of course. Never knew when to draw the line. Niece's nanny? Sure. Sister's ex? Nah. Brother's wife? Full fucking steam ahead."

She glanced at me, flashing me a wry smile.

"Lily's mine. Biologically. Not Alicia's. She told me there might be a mix up, and since you know about her, might as well know about me. I'm the piece of shit who knocked up her brother's wife on their anniversary because she was pissed at him. Instead of talking, I went straight to betraying his trust." She frowned at the road ahead.

"He loves Lily. No, *adores* her, cherishes every last second with her. It makes me sick sometimes, the guilt. I love Lily, but that night was a mistake. I never wanted to be a parent, but I'm glad if only for Enrique's sake. Still, I never touched Emilia again, not even when she made it clear Enri wanted to try for another. Once was enough. She got pregnant, and then she grew obsessed. Years, she still won't let it go. I see my family less and less, not just because I feel like shit for lying to my brother, but because she keeps making advances. Clearly she suspects there might be more to Alicia than meets the eye and is trying to go for her. But trust me, Ali wants her even less than I do."

I reeled at her words. *I made a big mistake. Will Alicia forgive me for doubting here?*

"She probably will."

I jumped and Ariana laughed.

"I can practically hear you thinking. Yes, Ali will forgive you. She loves you, as I'm sure you already know."

I blushed as I thought of all the ways she'd told me. No, she'd never said the actual words, but I knew.

I loved her too.

"Just be honest and open with her. She'll understand. However, little bit of advice?" Ariana turned as she pulled up beside a red motorcycle outside my door.

She got out of the car, leaving the keys in, and ducked her head though the window to see me.

"Our parents messed with all of our heads. And we left with some sort of baggage. Enri is painfully weak willed, I can't stand commitment, and Ali-" she paused. "Alicia has a thing with boundaries. It took her, what, six, seven months to talk to you? That's probably because you spoke to her first. She isn't going to show up unannounced, she won't blow up your phone more a couple times, and she'll always give you space for fear of making you fell how our parents made us feel. She'll open up herself to you but will wait forever for you to do the same. It's burned her in love more than a few times, so forgive me for interfering, but I had to be sure. If you don't wish to be with her, she'll respect that. Heck, she'll leave you be, like you never even met. But."

She fixed me a hard look.

"If you love her, go get her. Don't leave her in the dark like your parents did. Show her she's worth it being in someone's heart."

Alicia

"It was just a misunderstanding; she just needs time to think over what she saw. You know Emilia made it look bad."

After Ariana's calming words, I was able to think long enough to head back inside and grab my bag. Marcie had a somewhat abashed Emilia in some lost property shorts and an old t shirt of hers. It softened her, and I was annoyed by the spark of pity I felt for her. *If you cost me my relationship with Honey, pity will be the last thing on my mind.*

"So. Lily's teacher? That's who's got you all attentive and mushy? She's not strong enough for a Padrilla, is she? Running out at the sight of a little nudity."

I felt a wave of anger come over me. "You don't talk about her. Ever. You don't know a thing about Padrillas-if you did, you'd know we can be quite resentful."

"Oh please," Emilia scoffed. "I know two out of three. That's more than enough for me to sense a reoccurring trait in you all. Even Enri had a bit of passion when it came to the bedroom. In his prime, he was quite the stud. Little Miss Thing hardly has what it takes to handle a little foreplay let alone the real thing. And if you're anything like your sister…"

I cut her off angrily. "Don't think about me or my sister. I don't know what she saw in you to jump into your bed, but I know whatever it was, it's long gone. You stay away from me, Emilia. I love Lily, but you are a mess, and I hate that she's stuck with you as a mother right now." I watched her flinch but carried on, too heated from the look of betrayal on Honey's face.

"Get a grip, and a little self-restraint. You keep sniffing around like a dog in heat, and frankly, it's embarrassing to watch. Go home."

With that, I grabbed my stuff from my locker, nodded goodbye to a stunned Marcie, ignoring Emilia completely, as I made my way to my car. Within minutes I was home.

Entering my apartment brought a wave of emotions to the front of my mind. Pain mostly; every inch of my apartment held memories of our times together. Where we had our first date. Where we first kissed. Where we tried to bake apple custard pies for her class, but instead licked the custard from each other, only stopping when the oven beeped insistently. I entered my bathroom, wanting to take a shower to remove the floor polish from my hair, and Emilia's scent from my skin. I was assaulted by images of her first time fucking me.

She'd surprised me when she pulled it from her prim and proper schoolbag. I gaped at the purple ensemble, the cock large and veiny, not mention the bright bulbous artificial balls that swung heavily at the base, concealing the smaller vaginal insert that would stimulate her from within, ensuring her pleasure. Her eyes glowed as she told me of its vibration levels, all the while I could only stare at her in disbelief.

"Is it- it's too much, isn't it?" She'd asked bashfully.

"I mean- it's only our second date. It's a bit early to put out, what kind of girl do you take me for?" I teased. She rolled her eyes.

"Oh please, you were only too happy when I gave up my pussy on our first date. Bend over and let me have yours".

I laughed, already stripping, my cock eager even as my pussy clenched in anticipation. She made sure to give it a little kiss, French and dirty, before she quite literally bent me over at the counter.

Two head-pounding orgasms later, I couldn't help laughing.

"What's so funny?" She asked, out of breath.

"You-you, ah shit," I clutched my side as my laughter turned into a side stitch. "Have you been carrying that around in your bag all day?"

In the mirror's reflection, I saw her flush bright red, which set me off all over again. The purple dildo slid from my twitching pussy and my cock stiffened with an alarming intensity as I pictured all the other things I could encourage her to bring, or *wear* to school. What followed was a very long shower, followed by a trip to the bedroom. The next date was spent at hers, and I discovered Miss Honey Jane had quite the selection of toys, which were quickly put to good use.

I pushed past the memories, and took my shower, the quiet only amplifying my solitude.

I prepared a quick dinner, and sat on the couch, firmly ignoring memories of our first time, and indeed many other times on that very same couch. *I did nothing wrong. Honey was just confused. She just needs time to think. I will not wallow in my bed like a sorry teenager.*

I flicked through the television aimlessly, barely noticing as the room darkened with the setting sun.

A firm knock rang out and I banged my knee into the table in my eagerness to open it. I deflated at the sight of my neighbor holding out a small parcel for me. I thanked them and turned to close the door, noting Honey's name on the front.

"You can open it; it was for you."

I quickly spun round. Honey stood in the open elevator; her face flushed as her hands wrung together.

"Is it? My birthday isn't for a while longer." I opened the door wider in an open invitation. I stepped back as she stepped in, closing the door firmly behind her.

"It was for us, a mini anniversary present as it were."

I was intrigued, but I put it aside, too focused on her presence to think about gifts. I approached her cautiously, as she stood stiff with her arms wrapped around herself.

"Are you- would you like something to drink? Eat? I made-" I quickly checked my plate from earlier and grimaced. "Sandwiches."

Honey shook her head, but didn't move. The faint bubble of hope I felt at her presence threatened to pop with dread. I decided to bite the bullet.

"Are you looking to make a quick exit? I won't keep you here past whatever it is you have to say." It hurt to say those words, but I knew they were true. I knew all too well how it felt to be trapped.

"No! No, of course not. I just, I don't know where to start. And frankly," she blushed harder. "I'm embarrassed. About earlier. Running out, and assuming- about Lily."

I frowned down at the rug beneath my feet. "I understand. Why you left. It looked bad. Really bad, but I swear nothing happened, ever, and nothing *will* happen. Not with her, or anyone else." I wanted to pull her into my arms, but despite her words, I was still cautious. *An apology doesn't guarantee anything.*

I heard Honey step closer, and I met her gaze with guarded eyes.

They were red-rimmed, and my feet moved despite myself.

"What happened? Are you okay?"

Honey fell into my arms, and I gently sat us on the sofa, turning down the- architectural? - show that played in the background. Honey tucked her head beneath mine.

"I visited my parents today."

I tensed in surprise. *Did they now know about me? Were they disappointed she was not with a man?*

"My brother has a new baby. Another son."

I nodded slowly, trying to recall if she had ever mentioned this before. I remembered the first.

"Okay, that's good news. Everything went well? He's healthy?" I tried to think what could have made her upset.

"No. Well, yes, everyone is okay now, but Rachel nearly died. There were complications, and they removed half of her womb."

I rubbed her arm softly, trying to comfort her.

"That's good then. Unfortunate, but everyone is okay now, including baby, so that is very good news indeed."

I could barely hear her next words.

"What was that?"

"I didn't know."

My brows pulled together. "What didn't you know? About the complications?"

"I didn't know about any of it. My parents didn't tell me. Harry didn't call, and Rachel didn't send me a single word or anything."

My eyes widened in shock. "What? Why?"

"They thought I'd be jealous. Or, rather, my parents did. Because I was nearing the Change, still single and childless in a career that revolves around children. They thought I'd be a bitter old crone and cause unnecessary fuss around Rachel and the baby, so they didn't say a word. I only found out today by mistake."

I grew angry at the thought of her being singled out by her family.

"What kind of- "

"- Shit parents? Yeah, Ariana said the same thing."

I peered down at her. *in surprise*

"You met Ariana? When?"

Honey glanced up at me with a smirk.

"She was waiting for me outside my parents' home. Apparently where her little sister is concerned, she has no problems stalking her lovers."

I felt my face heat up. "Loca, she's absolutely mental. I'll talk to her-"

"No, no, it's fine. It was a good thing she was there to be honest, I was in no position to drive, so she brought me home. Gave me the talk, and convinced me to pull my head from my ass."

I started. "She didn't actually say that, did she?"

I'm going to kill her.

"Of course not, I was paraphrasing. She gave me the confidence to come here though. I'd probably have stayed home and moped on the couch indefinitely."

I winced.

"Alicia, she said you wouldn't have come, or called? At all. I that true?"

I colored slightly. "Yeah, probably. I don't want to overcrowd you, or come on too strong. I've already pushed enough. If ever you needed space, it was after thinking I was with Em- another woman."

"You're not crowding me. I love how direct and open you are. It helps me know where I stand, and more importantly, I feel like I can be safe with you." She pushed away, so she could meet my eyes fully, her blue eyes filling with tears once more. She blinked them back firmly. " I just found out my parents consider me a disappointing burden, to the point where they'd prefer to isolate me from the rest of the family, just to avoid the possibility of my failures tainting them. I spent the drive over here thinking about my life. About why it took me so long to see you, why I was so quick to run away, instead of staying and fighting for what I loved."

My breath hitched, but she wasn't done.

"All my life, I've felt like I'm on the fringe of something. I felt like my parents never truly loved me. Yes, I had food, clothes, they gave me so many opportunities that I know so many didn't. I *should* have been grateful, but all I felt was loneliness. My own *twin* felt like a stranger, we barely saw each other, and when we did, it was with a politeness I couldn't stand.

"Harry was born naturally, a smooth delivery I'm told, but I was 'difficult' and required a caesarean section. Apparently that carried on into my early years. While Harrison breastfed with ease, I struggled to latch and had to be bottle-fed. I developed colic, and had to be hospitalized, all the while he slept. Then I struggled with speech and walking, all the while he was hitting his milestones with ease. We should've been so close. Instead, he can't be asked to call me, not even when his wife is going through a difficult time. I always reached out first. With him, with my parents. Throughout last year, I never missed a call, but at no point could he be asked to mention the minor fact that his wife was expecting. Then, the *one* time I couldn't call because I was quite literally *sick to my stomach*- no one reaches out. Months later, I'm being kicked out of my childhood home for sins I didn't commit."

I tried to pull her in, my heart cracking at the wetness in her voice as she began to sob. But she pushed me away, shaking her head, although her hands stayed clenched around my shirt.

"I just wanted to them to care. To reach out, give me a hug, ask me how work is, not because of what their fancy friends say, but because they have a vested interest in me and my interests. You know, I only got into teaching because I wanted to impress my parents. Harry was in medical school, I thought I could be a lecturer like them. But I couldn't hack the doctorate program. Instead, with an early years master's degree and an unfinished doctorate, I turned to teaching. I could practically taste my parents' disappointment. It was only when I switched to the kindergarten that they even bothered to learn what school I taught at.

"I tried to impress them by getting married, and having children, like a good traditional woman does. Instead, my relationships failed, and I soon lost interest in continuing to date and getting my heart broken. I felt like I was on the side, watching life rush past as I tried desperately to hold onto something, the kids, my work- *anything*."

Honey was sobbing outright, and I pulled her into me, ignoring her faint attempts to push me away. I held her tight, pressing my lips repeatedly into her hair.

I love you, I love you, I love you so much, Honey.

"You've got me, you hear? I'm right here, holding onto you, as long as you want me. I'm right here."

"I convinced myself being a doting housewife was the way forward, and felt like shit every time things didn't work out."

"Fuck that shit, fuck them all, baby. You're perfect as you are."

This time, when she pulled away, I let her, making sure to keep her on my lap. She held my face in her hands, pressing her lips softly against mine.

"It wasn't till I had given up, on all of it, everything my parents had wanted from me, when I was sure it was all over, that my life was over- only then was I able to see you. And I fell, hard. No questions about what they would approve or disapprove of, no longing for what I *should* need. Instead, I threw myself into the gorgeous Latina in the sexy sweats, and she caught me. You," she kissed me harder, and I pulled her in tighter, feeling tears prickling in my own eyes.

"You were everything to me, and still, you've managed to make every dream come true."

I watched in confusion as she brought her hands to mine, pulling them to rest above her womb.

"I'm pregnant." She whispered against my lips, and I stilled completely.

Wait.

I was barely conscious of the tears rolling down my face.

"You're- *truly?* I'm- you're-? Holy *shit*!"

I whooped loudly, lifting her into my arms, dancing around the room as she cried into my shoulder, laughing wetly. I couldn't believe it.

"I know I always said I would do it, put a baby in you but- *holy shit*!"

"We'll need to watch our potty mouths, yours especially," Honey said with a flick to my ear. I bit hers in retaliation.

"Fuck that. I told you, our kids aren't getting that fucked up sanitized childhood of yours, nor the open fuckery of mine. Nope, they're gonna swear, and put their boundaries up, and we're gonna let them express their every emotion whenever they want."

Honey snorted incredulously. "Not whenever they want, they'll be spoiled rotten. Are you going to make me be the bad parent?"

"None of us will be the bad parents. We'll both be awesome, and if the kids want something on of us disagree with, we'll take turns fucking each other silly, and whoever wins gets the final say." I said, feeling my dick rapidly stirring, as if to celebrate with us.

"That's not fair, you've had more experience in that department, you'll win every time."

I leered at her, a wicked smirk on my face.

"Oh, I plan on it. But Honey, if you want more experience, I'm your very willing test subject."

Honey

I nervously adjusted my dress, and checked my hair once more in the mirror, checking the curls were keeping their shape.

Today was the last day of school and although my class wouldn't be here for the whole day, I wanted pop in before their trip. I checked my bump wasn't visible beneath the light fabric. Despite only being fourteen weeks along, I was surprised to discover the small but firm bump that had sprouted out, almost overnight. Alicia had been ecstatic in the two weeks following our discovery, but the day she had noticed our little baby's bump revealed a level of joy I'd yet to have seen.

We were keeping the news quiet till our first scan, which was scheduled for midday today with Dr. Kudira, after which we'd decided to tell the family. They were

Alicia's

having a family barbeque to celebrate the end of Lily's kindergarten years, and her birthday, as she would be spending the actual day at Disneyland-Paris. world

Strong arms slipped around my waist, soft breasts pressing into my back as those muscles flexed and hands found their way to my growing bust, squeezing firmly. I moaned as Alicia found my sensitive nipples, pressing firmly. *If I thought her insatiable before…*

"We don't have time for this, Ali," I moaned out, even as I pressed back into her firm length. "Please…"

"Please stop? Ah, well since you asked so nicely." Alicia let her hands slide away and I all but whined as she chuckled softly into my ear. "Sorry baby, you're right, we're going to be late for Lily's last day, and you'd never forgive yourself if you didn't see the kids off for the summer."

"Fuck you, for starting something you can't finish." I muttered with a pout.

I kept up my childish mood on the way to school, evading her kiss as she dropped me off. She laughed as I shooed her away, promising to pick me up for eleven-thirty.

I wore a small smile even as I cursed her for getting me revved up, too distracted to notice Robert sliding up to me, walking in step.

"Morning Honey, you're looking delightful today."

I tried not to sigh too loudly. He *was* taking my class on the trip after all. "Thank you, Robert. And thank you for the trip, for stepping in. You really were a hero."

His chest puffed out proudly, and I bit back a smile as he postured beside me. "Ah, but of course. Happy to help. And hey, if you want, we can catch a drink afterwards? Catch-up before we break for summer?"

I decided now might as well be the time to announce it to him, I'd already put in my leave with the principal.

Three years of paid maternity leave, 2 years for paternity leave, not that Alicia was taking much time. Marcie had kept her so busy with the gym, she felt bad about leaving her completely. Instead, she'd cut back on hours, as to not leave Marcie completely in the lurch.

"My partner and I are expecting, Robert. No drinks for me unfortunately."

I expected him to react with a sense of male entitlement, yet his face transformed completely. "*Oh,*" he breathed, his eyes shining. "*Bless you*, I- congratulations Honey. That is blessed news."

I found myself genuinely giving him a smile. "Thank you, Robert. So, you see, I really do appreciate this. The stress would've-"

"Don't even finish the thought!" Robert shuddered. He shoos me off to my classroom, where I could hear the chattering of my students, all early for the trip. They got quiet as I came in. I felt tears prickling my eyes already.

"Oaky," I started. "I hope you guys know this has been the biggest year of my life. You guys are amazing, intelligent, you all have the potential to do so much, I hope you continue to push yourselves. Also-" I couldn't help but cry, and a chorus of *awws* filled the room, followed by little bodies moving in and pulling me down to a hug.

I hugged as many students as I could in one sitting, before I gave them each individual hugs and kisses. When I got to Lily, the poor child was sobbing harder than me.

"Lily, sweetheart, it'll be alright."

"It won't!" She wailed, clinging onto me.

"Of course it will," I cooed. "It'll be a bit scary, but you won't be alone. You'll have your friends, you parents, your teachers. You'll absolutely smash it!"

"But I don't want another teacher, I want *you.*"

I almost laughed, but I knew she wouldn't understand. Instead, I whispered to her, "You'll have me. Just not as you teacher. But trust me, I'll be there to help you should you need it, sweetie."

"Promise?" I smiled softly.

"Pinky promise."

She beamed at me, and I couldn't help beaming back, before my arms were full of another child. By the time the goodbyes were done, Susan's pinched face filled the doorway.

"It's time to go." She announced, and I helped get the kids in line for the last time this year, blinking back tears. Yes, this had been the best year, and it would likely be the last for a little while. Most women started maternity leave as soon as they confirmed their pregnancy, to ensure a peaceful gestation period with minimal stress. I wanted to start the new school year, but by September I'd be at five months. I'd only get a handful of months before leaving for almost three years. It wasn't the best choice.

I'd already began looking at hobbies I may wish to take up to pass the time not working. I began to pack my personal affairs and decorations, leaving spare pens and materials for the next teacher. Time flew past as I sorted through what I wanted to keep, donate to the next class or throw away.

"Well, I hope you're proud of yourself."

If the kids made me want to stay, Susan made me glad to leave. I finished loading my crate container before facing her.

"Is that so? Why, Susan?" I crossed my arms.

"You got to sweet talk a man into taking your place, on a trip that was catered to you, just so you could dress nice and go on dates. How utterly self and frankly, manipulative."

I almost laughed. Instead, I nodded slowly before I continued packing. Just like my parents, some people weren't worth wasting breath on.

"Nothing to say for yourself? Typical. You know, I never liked you. I hate your type, all delicate and sweet, batting your eyes at every man that passes, but you're the worst of them Even your *name*. Honey. What kind of ridiculous name is that? You just slide through while the rest of us have to pull our way through, and you get to get everyman to do your bidding. It's disgusting and un-feminist. I daresay women like you are the reason the birthrate went down, ruining innocent families-"

"*I beg your mighty pardon?!*"

I whipped around at the sound of my partner's livid voice. Besides her was my boss, who wore the same look of horror and disgust.

Susan stuttered and stammered her way through an excuse, but the damage was done.

"Did you just tell my girlfriend she was responsible for the Change, while insinuating she used sexual favors to manipulate men into being *nice?*"

"I- I- It was a-"

"Harassing her for months wasn't enough? You had to get a few more insults in? Honey has run herself *ragged* for her students, and all you can see is her beauty and kindness, which should be virtues, but you can't seem to see them that way, Fine. *But what makes you think verbally assaulting a pregnant woman was the right call?*"

I almost felt bad as the blood drained from Susan's face. Her eyes flickered between my stomach and the principal's foreboding expression with more panic.

"I didn't know! I didn't- you didn't say you were *pregnant!*"

"Is that what you call an excuse, *Susan*?! Unbelievable! My office! NOW!"

Susan jumped and scampered out with nary a backwards glance, the principal. Meanwhile, I kept my gaze on the Amazon gracing my classroom with her beauty.

And passion. My pussy gave a wanting throb, reminding me of our unfinished business from earlier.

There is a desk. And no one should be coming by, they'll be finishing their class clearance or going on various trips. Anyway, I've got three years paid leave before they can fire me even if they do catch us. Fuck, I'm doing it.

I slowly made my way towards my unsuspecting girlfriend, father of the child currently nestled in my womb. My panties were beyond drenched, and I wondered whether you could hear the sticky noise I could. ~~feel~~ *~ stickiness I felt*

"Unbelievable, what a *bitch*. I can't *believe* she said – what are you doing?"

I looked up from my perch on the floor in front of her, my fingers continuing towards her jean shorts. *I don't know why Alicia in denim is so fucking hot, but no complaints. Zero. Nada. Zilch.*

"*The door is still fucking open!*" She hissed, peering down at me, her fingers helping mine, even as she glanced furtively towards the door.

Medoth thinks the lady protests too much.

I smirked up at her. "My, my, what happened to the girl who said, '*I beg your mighty pardon*'?"

A ruddy color hit her cheeks.

"I've been trying to watch the language, but since you don't care for it- *you better not let one fucking drop escape your mouth, slut.*"

I whined hard, gorging myself on her long cock, dimly remembering to breathe through my nose, with my lips over my teeth as Alicia had taught me.

Of course, it's easier to take a fat cock into your throat when you're hanging over the side of the bed, with your partner pumping away steadily, two fingers keeping your pussy filled as you did so.

On your knees is a different story.

Still, I swallowed inch after inch down like a jumbo hotdog, moaning deliriously as she nudged the base of my throat. I hummed, enjoying the vibrations pressing against her cock. Evidently so did Alicia, as she couldn't help thrusting roughly once or twice into my mouth.

When I felt myself grow lightheaded, practically dozing and drooling on that magnificent length, I pulled back regrettably. Alicia fell back against the class door, rubbing rough hands over her face with a muffled curse., her cock bobbing violently, red, uncut, ruddy and most certainly ready.

"Yes, we should have shave stopped, good. Fine. Well done, baby, you got me back goo-"

Alicia froze behind me, and I smirked at the reason why.

Whilst she had lingered by the door, I used her distraction to slip out of my knickers. I was currently crawling towards the far desk where we'd first 'met'. I knew her strangled sound was a reaction to my exposed ass and pussy, slowly rocking over to my chosen spot. Once there, I took a deep breath before arching my back like a cat, shaking my rump like a cat in heat, trying to entice my tomgirl into rearranging my guts.

"Oh *Honey*, you sexy thing, you're playing with fire here."

"I just *need* you, Ali."

Silence.

Just as I felt shame start to take over, tainting the moment. I was about to get up, when I felt the soft wet glide of a tongue over my dripping snatch. I let out a violent whine as I tried to twist away, but her thick hands gripped my hips tightly. She kept me there, prostrate on the floor for two leg-weakening orgasms, before I next heard her speak.

"Well, well, well. What have we here? A naughty little sexpot bent over and dripping just for me."

"*PLEASE.*"

I was eager for it, but when her dick punched in, all the breath left my lungs, and I grunted my way through a choppy orgasm. Ali didn't even hesitate. She continued to pound me into the desk, each hit pressing against that spot, causing me to squirt in no time, drenching the carpet beneath me.

She wrestled me onto my front completely across the ladybug rug, and despite my meagre attempts at turning around, she kept me in place with a glorious flex of those muscles.

I could faintly hear my principal heading back this way, but he was waylaid by another teacher. Before I could warn Ali, she pulled me away from the ~~desk~~ floor, before spreading me open on the desk.

"Fuck yes baby," she said, before she resumed the furious pace, pushing me into my third orgasm. Ali swore roughly proceeding to empty her load deep inside me, where her cock was nestled against the opening of my womb. She fell into me for a second, before she pulled out, letting her come drip down my legs.

Holy crap.

We were able to tidy ourselves up very quickly and my boss wished us the best as we came out, minutes later.

The drive was spent in silence as we thought of what just happened. Alicia pulled into the hospital car lot and killed the ignition. She stared right ahead, before turning to face me.

"I don't – I- Nope, no words. Wow."

With that eloquent speech, we were off, heading inside the building. I excused myself to the bathroom as Alicia filled out the papers. I cleaned up my *area* as best as I could, but I felt certain the doctor would know.

Ah well. It just means we're passionate. We all know how we got here.

I joined her and helped her fill out a couple of questions before we were called.

Dr Kudira was just as tall as I remembered, a few inches below Alicia, her blue hair almost glowing in the lights. Her smile was just as open and inviting as before.

Alicia's hand was warm in mine as we sat in the softly lit exam room, the low hum of the ultrasound machine filling the silence. My first official prenatal appointment. Three months along. I'd been told this was the "dating scan," the one where they check the baby's size, heartbeat, and development.

Dr. Kudira smiled as she wheeled her stool closer, but her eyes were sharp, assessing. "How have you been feeling emotionally?" she asked, almost casually, as she prepped the transducer with gel.

I hesitated. "Tired. A bit queasy. But… okay."

"And your support system?" she continued. "Do you have family nearby? Friends you can rely on?"

Alicia squeezed my hand, answering for us. "We've got each other. And some friends. Why?"

Dr. Kudira just nodded, jotting something down. "And financially? Are you both in stable work?"

Alicia's brow furrowed. "Wait—are you… screening us?"

The doctor didn't flinch. "In a way, yes. Over the last decade, we've seen too many parents become overwhelmed or unfit to care for their children. The consequences for the child can start before birth—stress, neglect, lack of preparation. We now take steps to minimize that risk from the earliest point possible."

Her tone was matter of fact, but it made my stomach twist. "So, you're deciding if we're… worthy?" I asked, my voice sharper than I intended.

"It's not about worth," she said evenly. "It's about readiness. Having a child is no longer as readily available an option as it once was. With so many fertility treatments failing, natural conceptions are a precious coupling, and we want to make sure it reflects the level of care and support the child will be exposed to. Too often in the past, people in terrible situations are able to procreate, and *keep* those infants, resulting in damaged individuals believed to have contributed to the current state of affairs. It really is just protocol."

I shifted on the exam bed, suddenly wanting to get up. "I don't like this. I want to leave."

Alicia nodded immediately. "If you're uncomfortable, we can find another doctor."

Dr. Kudira's expression softened, but her voice stayed firm. "You can, but this protocol is implemented in every hospital. You'll face the same questions elsewhere. At least… see your baby before you decide."

I looked at Alicia. She gave me a small, encouraging smile. Reluctantly, I lay back again.

The gel was cold against my skin, and then the probe pressed lightly over my lower belly. The screen flickered to life.

And there it was.

A tiny, perfect shape, curled in on itself, a flicker of movement where the heart was beating. My throat tightened.

"Our little bee," Alicia whispered, her eyes shining. My breath hitched at the name. *Bee*.

Dr. Kudira adjusted the angle, her own smile growing. "Well," she said, tilting her head, "it looks like your little bee has... a twin."

I blinked at her. "A twin?"

She chuckled. "Yes. Two bees in the hive. Double the joy, double the nappies."

Alicia laughed, a sound half-shocked, half-delighted. I just stared at the screen, my heart pounding in time with theirs—two tiny heartbeats, steady and strong.

It was even more than I'd expected.

"I can't believe we made them." Alicia whispered, and we kissed gently, all thoughts of our doctor forgotten.

"I realize you may still be uncomfortable," Dr. Kudira said, "But I just need a couple of medical questions for your baby's chart. You can pass on to any doctor afterwards."

I was still hesitant, but I nodded. *Anything for our little bumblebees.*

"These are for you, other mommy."

Alicia nodded.

"Now I don't mean to be indelicate, but you are transgender, I believe?"

Alicia stilled.

"Please know that these are purely medical, for the health of the child. I'm required to ask what hormonal treatment you are taking. These could have impact on the children's development, and-"

"None! No medication. I just- I cross-dress. I'm in drag right now."

Dr. Kudira stared at us silently for a moment, before closing the open files on her computer. She swiveled back around to face us.

"I hope the two of you realize I am on your side. I was a doctor before the worst of this 'Change' went down. I studied the falling figures, I was part of the volunteering trials, and research teams. There's been a lot of work and red tape up into these sorts of things, just to ensure the safety, welfare and happiness of the future of the human race. It is estimated that if the birth rates remain this low, in thirty years, over half of humanity will be gone. We are trying to prevent that. All this to say- please do not lie to me. It's not safe for you, mommy, or for your babies."

I stared back at the doctor uneasily.

"She's telling the truth, she takes no medication, aside from the odd paracetamol."

Dr. Kudira's eyes narrowed, but she sighed. "Okay. I've had three copies printed, the nurse at reception should have them. I'll understand if you choose a different doctor. I wish you best the same."

We left the examination room silently, lost in our thoughts. I was worried about our 'screening' questions. We *were* prepared. So what we didn't have everything perfectly in place yet. We at least had the discussion of moving in. The gift I'd gotten Ali for our half anniversary had been a key to my place. It was far from perfect, but it had more room, especially for two infants, although we'd need to stat house searching.

"You don't think she'll focus on the whole medication thing, do you?"

Alicia looked concerned. I kissed her cheek to soften her up. "I don't think so. Besides if it comes down to more, we'll just admit to a sperm doner."

Alicia looked hesitant.

"What is it?" I asked.

"I know she made you uncomfortable, but- and remember it all comes down to who *you* feel secure with, but-"

I sighed and interrupted her gently.

"I want Dr. Kudira too. I liked her even before, but the questioning did terrify me. The thought of getting questions wrong by mistake, and them simply being able to take away our child-"

Alicia shushed me gently. "Woah there, Nervous Nells. No one is taking our babies. And even if they tried, we'd teach them fairly quickly that you don't mess with Padrillas."

My chest warmed. "I'm not a Padrilla, Alicia."

She led me from the office with a knowing grin.

"Not yet, you aren't. But that's easily remedied."

Alicia

"Will they like me?" Honey asked, not for the first time.

"Of that, you can be sure. Emilia will be strange, but you can just ignore her."

I tugged my girlfriend's hand along with me, as we entered the large foyer of Enri's home. In just a few weeks, it had changed radically. I don't know what conversation Ariana had with Emilia shortly after Honey and I reconciled, but the ex-model had been so quiet and unassuming the last couple of weeks, I hardly knew what to make of it. Her eccentric décor had been toned down and I swore I saw her drop Lily off in jeans and a large t-shirt, a pair of crocs on her feet. I didn't question it past a quick question to Ariana. When she told me I didn't want to know, I believed her.

Ariana could be quite the formidable opponent when crossed.

Speaking of-

"Hey again, Honey. Glad your head made it here okay, I was sure you'd left it behind when you left me behind, ~~that~~ time."

Honey laughed and blushed, and I scowled as my sister enveloped her in a tight hug as we moved into the open front den.

"Easy, Ari. Give her room to breathe," came Enrique's quiet rebuke as he turned the corner, Lily in his arms as always. She squealed running to hug Honey, and ~~hardly~~ clung ~~away~~, even as Marcie appeared from the kitchen. When the two loudly began squalling over the new yoga corner of the gym, I felt myself check out, feeling bad for the five-year-old kid caught in the middle of the excitement. Lastly, Emilia emerged, dressed in a beige crocheted lounge set that covered her, from neck to ankle. I blinked in surprise. She looked so open and ~~vulnerable~~, you'd never have guessed how extreme her behavior had gotten.

"Hello, Alicia." Everyone paused, waiting for the other greeting. Enri cleared his throat pointedly, and Emilia grimaced. "Hi, Honey. No, sorry, it's weird. Class just finished and she's already home sucking up to everyone with her little 'helpless' act. She isn't even *meant* to be here."

Several things happened at one; Ariana threw her hands up on in exasperation and Enri flushed violently. But it was Lily who stole the show.

"Mama why are you being rude! Miss Janey is the best. She's kind, she's fun, and she always keeps her promises, unlike *you*."

Emilia gaped at her daughter.

"She said she was going to be here, and now you're making her sad! You make everyone sad! I hate you, *I hate you!*"

With that, she ran off, tears streaming down her face. Honey gave me a concerned look, before rushing after her, leaving the Padrilla's (Marcie quietly excused herself in search of a drink) in the den.

Emilia was still in shock. Enri spoke first.

"I warned you, Emilia. I warned you not to cause a scene."

Emilia returned to herself, scowling despite herself. "You *warned* me? Am I a child, to be told how to behave, to be told off, and *warned?* I made a minor comment-"

"There shouldn't have been one! I asked you to refrain yourself, for your daughter's sake, but you couldn't keep it in for just one afternoon! Does *nothing* matter to you?"

"Oh please, Enri, stop being so dramatic. Lily is just throwing a tantrum, I expect *someone's* been spoiling her."

"I give her affection! Show her love, and make sure she knows she has at least one parent willing to give her everything they are. What do you do? Wear your fancy clothes and noisy heels, before stomping all over her little heart with your careless words. Did you even *think* about discussing things before you fired Jessica?"

Emilia waved him off. "That *slut?* Of course not. She spent her days fucking and playing around instead of actually *caring* for Lily-"

"She wasn't the only one!"

I hissed in shock, and apparently, I wasn't the only one reeling from Enri's uncharacteristically harsh words. Ariana's face drained, the only sign of the fear she must've felt at his words. Emilia recovered quickly, firing back, "What? Did you get a piece of her as well? Is that why you're so mad about that useless-"

"I know you had an affair."

Across the room, Aria's jaw clenched, but she didn't move a muscle.

Emilia stammered her way through a denial, but Enri cut her off. His normally pale face was red with anger.

"I found your horny texts, begging for a repeat, your pictures, *videos*, some taken in the same room as Lily! You had so little care for me or her, and frankly, I don't know if I can stand it much longer!"

I could only watch the emotions play out between the two, noting Ariana's faintly trembling for in the background. *You ever hear that saying about chickens coming to roost, Ari? Jessica was one chick too many, opened up a can of worms for the others.*

"Enri. Enri- it meant- it was just the one time!"

"I saw you come home in that trench coat the other week. What happened the? Because I didn't see you come to *me*, and the sky was a clear blue, not a cloud in the vicinity Where did you go, *Emmy*?"

Emilia's eyes darted to mine in a rare pleading gaze. I took pity on her.

"She came to the gym. She heard about Marcie's difficult investor, and I thought a little eye candy could help."

Sorry Marcie.

Enri's soulful eyes bet mine, gazing intently, before a small frown settled in the center of his brows.

"Okay. You were trying to *help*."

"Enrique, what did you mean, 'you're *done?*"

I wondered the very same thing.

"I meant what I said. I'm sick of this limbo. You want me but you don't actually want *me*, just the pansy who followed you around campus, all those years ago. You love me, but you betray our vows and what's worse, you're itching to do it again. I won't do it. I won't be that pansy anymore. I- "

We all waited to see if he would finish that sentence the way we all thought he would.

"I don't want to upset Lily any more than you already have. It's over, but I- I don't want to divorce you. Let's go on as we have. Separately, in a marriage we can't afford to break." Emilia looked crushed, which surprised me. I was sure she didn't actually care for my brother, was there out of a sense of duty, and the financial perks of being a married couple with a biological child.

"W-will you-?" Emilia clasped her arms around herself, slowly rocking herself in disbelief. Enri scoffed.

"So, you can stray when we were in a committed relationship, but I can't even when we're separated?"

Emilia flinched and shook her head in sharp jerks.

"Yeah, well. I'm not living by these one-sided rules of marriage. Tit for tat, Emilia. Remember that. Oh, and, just in case you get any ideas-"

He whirled to look her dead in the eye and snarled, "You try any sneaky custody shit, and I'll have you buried under so much litigation, you won't know which way's up. Lily is *mine*."

With that, he went after his daughter. Ariana and I were left utterly gob smacked, even as Marcie slid back in with a grimly impressed expression. Emilia stood there a second longer, before hurrying up the stairs, not even sparing Ariana a glance.

"Holy shit." I whispered.

There was no response until Honey walked back in, walking into my arms. "What happened?" She asked, but I shook my head slightly. *Not here,* I communicated, and she nodded softly.

"So. Um. We actually had news. It's why we came so early." Honey eyed me in exasperation, but I shrugged. I figured we may as well continue the plan, even if everything was falling apart. It seemed like there would hardly be a *good* time after that display.

"I'm pregnant. With twins." Honey interjected, probably sensing I was at a loss as to how to continue.

Faint congratulations trailed in, but I didn't take it personally, and knew Honey wouldn't either. Everyone was in shock. The true excitement would come with time. Speaking of…

"So, we're going to head out. We've got one more stop today."

Honey eyed me questioningly, but I didn't clarify her further. confusion. *This last one was- impulsive.*

"Call me- Ari." I called her, making sure to catch her eye. "Call me." She nodded absentmindedly.

I waved at Marcie and called out a hasty farewell to Enri as he re-entered with Lily nowhere to be found. *Asleep,* Enri mouthed, and I nodded into the quick hug I gave him.

"Love you guys," I said, grabbing and kissing Honey's hand *I* we made our way to the car.

For the next few minutes, there was silence. Suddenly Honey exclaimed-

"What *happened* when I left? Why was the mood so- *off*?"

I shook my head silently. After a moment, Honey spoke again.

"Did Enri find out? About Ariana and Emilia?"

I frowned. "Not quite? He knew she had cheated on him, but not with *who*. He said they're over, but he won't get divorced, so Lily has some sense of stability. I don't even get it. I've never seen him like that."

Honey nodded slowly. "Sometimes even the calmest people are pushed to the brink."

"I guess so. I just know Ariana's going to be in a bit of a state. She felt like shit before, but *this?* Yeah, it's going to be a long year for us."

"They've got to tell him."

I glanced at her in shock. "You think so? He's already taking this- not *well*, how would finding out about Ariana's betrayal fix that?"

Honey shrugged. "It's going to suck for a long time, but she can't let it linger over them all for much longer. That's what led to all this in the first place."

She was right. But was it so awful of me to wish they'd wait until our bumblebees were at least born? I worried about how the stress of the family drama would change things. And on that note of family drama, I pulled up to the address Ariana gave me.

Honey glanced out of the window, first in curiosity, then shock, and finally horror.

"Ali, why are we at my parents' house? How did you even- damn it, Ariana."

I grimaced along with her. I wasn't thrilled for this either, but Ariana had pointed out, perhaps in a burst of foresight, that my family was already small and screwed up. Making it smaller over miscommunications was a mistake I wasn't keen to repeat, particularly after the display from earlier.

Honey had a wild panicked look about her.

"Honey, baby. It'll be okay. We go in, tell them, and if they want nothing more, we leave it. But we've got to go in."

"Why?" She asked in a small voice. I placed my palm over her small mound.

"Don't you want to be able to tell our little bees you tried everything to get them the family we didn't?"

Because I did.

Honey

For the second time this year, I was at my parents' house. Uninvited, once again. But not alone.

Alicia stood just behind me, her arms caging me against her front, her hands rested on my soft stomach, and she pressed kisses to the back of my head as we waited for our knocks to be answered. It had been a few minutes now, and even though it was a balmy summer eve, I shivered. Alice gently caressed my arms, trying to smooth away the goosebumps that rose.

"If they don't answer in the next minute, we'll leave."

I looked up at her, smiling at the clear displeasure on her face.

"What happened to telling our children we did everything to make it work? You can't leave without camping out on their front porch."

"I'm ready to admit defeat already. I said we *tried*; it doesn't have to be a success story."

I giggled, and she smiled, her eyes softening, and she pulled me in for a kiss.

The door opened abruptly, and we jumped apart, although it was quite obvious what we'd been up to. My father's stern expression greeted us, and he pressed his lips tightly.

I found myself speechless, the nerves of what to say rushing back to me.

I was at my strait-laced parents' home, in the arms of my girlfriend, who had just knocked me up with her 100 percent female phallus.

Even if I removed that last tidbit, we had lesbian relationship, child out of wedlock, child of unknown (as far as they knew) origins, and that was not including the public display of affection we'd almost engaged in.

We've got a full house of conservative bingo.

When it became clear my father had no plans on starting the conversation, Alicia took the reins.

"Hello sir. You know your daughter. My name is Alicia Padrilla, and your daughter and I-"

"-Are roommates!" I squeaked, at once regretting my loose lips. *Roommates indeed, as if he didn't see us almost to lock lips right in front of the door. Fix this, Honey!*

"I mean, we live together. Occasionally. Soon to be permanently. Maybe, - if she- you- want?" I turned to Alicia mid-speech, and she wasn't even mad, just faintly amused.

"I do want, but I thought introducing myself as you girlfriend would have been enough for now. But hey, if there are any more relationship milestones you like us to hit out here on your childhood doorstep?"

"I'd rather you didn't move your relationship forward while the door is open. The air-conditioning in Florida cost a bitch and a half.

I blushed furiously, turning back to my father, who'd stepped to let us in. This time I was led straight to the living room, no hiding us, or pretending they weren't entertaining their favourite child and his accomplishments.

I took a deep breath before entering, and Alicia pressed another kiss to the top of my head, reminding me I wasn't alone and heartbroken this time. I squared my shoulders and entered the room, leaving intertwined with Ali's.

My brother was absent this time, probably on a work call, and my nephews were both awake and set out on the large cream rug that dominated the minimalistic room. My mother sat perched awkwardly beside Rachel, tapping her leg. The image reminded me of a dog being pet by its owner. Only, judging by Rachel's face, the dog didn't appreciate the overflowing affection.

I could feel Alicia's slip from my hand to the small of my back as we stepped into the living room. The air was thick with that brittle politeness my family specialized in.

I cleared my throat. "Hi. Er- we... have some news."

Mom's eyes narrowed, but she didn't speak.

I took a breath. "Before I say it, I need to acknowledge something. The last time I was here, I found out—by accident—that you'd all kept Harry and Rachel's pregnancy from me. And the birth. And that it was complicated. That hurt. A lot. And I still don't understand why no one thought I deserved to know. I -" My breath caught, but I pressed on. "I haven't been the most forward, I could have made the effort to go to Jacksonville, but I have reached out every time we've spoken, and the one-time I physically couldn't, no one reaches out to me either."

Mom's gaze slid away as Harry slipped back into the room, his jaw tightening as he saw us.

"I'm not saying this to pick a fight," I continued, "but to make it clear that I don't want to go through Mom, Dad, to see my nephews. Harry, Rachel. If you ever want to visit, or hang out, you can call me directly. No middleman."

Mom's voice cut in, sharp and dismissive. "Oh, for heaven's sake, Honey. This is just another one of your attention-seeking performances. Same as when you were a child. We didn't tell you because you wouldn't understand . You don't have children, likely you never will. The Change is right around the corner, and you bring home a *woman*. What aid could you have been, regurgitating whatever WebMD throws at you. The best they could've hoped for is a babysitter, but you are so weird with Jacoby. You barely hold him; ~~you flinch at his cries instead of handling them.~~

Honestly. I was doing them a favor, and in truth, I did you a favor as well. No point being reminded about what you can't have. You were always such a strange child, and I didn't want to hear about you having a *crisis,* although it looks as if you already have."

The room was silent. Even Harry's stoic impression slipped. Before I could respond, Alicia stepped forward, her voice calm but edged with steel. "What a despicable woman. Unbelievable. Using the actions of a child who felt neglected against her all these years later. Not the actions of the woman standing here now—a woman with a good job, a strong support system, and a partner who never fails to show her love."

"What does love have to do with it? If you want to live your hippy free-love life, no one will stop you. You're a grown woman, as your friend tells me. I just want you to remember my words when you see everyone around you get serious, have children an-"

"I'm pregnant."

Mom scoffed. "There you go again, always a new story with you. The home pregnancy kits are no longer effective at detecting the true pregnancy hormone. Harry, tell your sister-"

"I'm three months along, just had my first scan," I continued, speaking over her, feeling my heart pound furiously as I did, bracing for her disappointment. Alicia remained a solid weight behind me. My mother squinted at my midriff, leaning forward as if to deliver another blow, but Dad's voice broke in. "Do you have any pictures?"

The shift caught me off guard. I reached into my pocket- no purse, no flowers, certainly no wine; all I had in my hands to give was the grainy images of my babies in the white envelope. I handed him the glossy black-and-white print.

His eyes softened instantly. He traced the outline with his thumb, and I saw the tear before he wiped it away.

"Wait, is that- I'm a little rusty, but that's two? Am I right? Harry! Get over here. That's two, right? Twins?" Harry nodded in shock, his eyes flicking to mine.

"Twins."

My father had crossed over to us. Reaching out, he shook Alicia's hand firmly. Then he turned to me. "I'm sorry for going along with your mother's idea. I should have spoken up. I hope you'll reconsider cutting us out of the children's lives... but I won't press you. These babies are going to need all the calm and stability they can get. Absolutely no stress- even from us."

I nodded, my throat too tight to speak.

"We should probably head out," Alicia cut in.

"Okay," my father coughed to clear his throat, before gingerly hugging me. I felt my own tears pool and fall down my face. I couldn't remember the last time I'd been hugged by him. *And to think, I wouldn't have had the opportunity, without...*

Alicia.

As we stepped toward the door, ignoring my mother's spluttering behind us, Rachel appeared from the hallway, her expression cautious. "Hey... would you two like to get lunch tomorrow? Just us?" She shrugged awkwardly. "A girl's date?"

I glanced at Alicia, who gave me a small nod and wry smile. "Yeah," I said. "I'd like that."

"I mean, we may have to invite the kids, or at least Rory, but he can't talk, so the sanctity of girls' night is safe!"

We laughed, and as if right on cue, Rory let out a loud cry, as if sensing his mother joking about leaving him behind.

Outside, the air felt cooler, lighter. We walked toward the car, and halfway we were stopped again, this time by Harry. I saw Rachel still in the doorway, now a babbling Rory.

"Hey. Look, I won't pretend this isn't awkward, but- seeing the scan, seeing your *twins*. It got me thinking. We could make more of an effort. And hey, you guys are welcome to Jacksonville whenever you want. In fact," He dug into his pocket, pulling out a business card. "This has every one of my and Rachel's cells. Our work cell, private, anything at all. If you want a new doctor, or have any questions, or anything at all, please call."

"Thank you, Harry."

He grinned, a stiff grin, but it held. "No problem. Twins have got to stick together, right?" With that he headed back to Rachel, picking up a waving Jacoby.

I stopped before we continued down the drive, choosing to turn, and kiss Alicia. Behind us, Rachel let out a whoop of approval.

I smiled into the kiss, thinking—not for the first time—
how lucky I was to have found her, and how I was very
much looking forward to forever together.

Take a sneak peek at the next story...

Hanna Rose, Saucy Seductress

The office was quiet in that way it only ever was after nine p.m.—the hum of the air conditioning, the faint tick of the wall clock, the occasional groan of the building settling. My monitor's glow painted the desk in cold light, the half-drunk coffee beside me long since gone bitter.

The project in front of me wasn't due for another two weeks, but Hanna wanted to "see where it was at" so she could decide whether it was worth greenlighting. Which meant she wanted it finished. Now.

Hanna. God, I loathed her. Not in the fiery, dramatic way you hate someone who's wronged you, but in the slow-burn way you hate someone who takes pleasure in flexing their power over the smallest, most meaningless things. She'd make me redo a report because the font "felt too casual," or hold back approval on a budget until I'd "reconsidered the tone" of an email. It wasn't about the work—it was about reminding me she could.

And the worst part? I recognized it. That itch for control. That satisfaction in pulling the strings. I'd told myself I was nothing like her, but the truth was, I'd used that same instinct before.

My fingers stilled on the keyboard.

It had been only a couple of months ago, but it still felt raw. Alicia and Honey had come to the house—Honey was glowing these days, honey locks flowing, belly rounded—to announce their pregnancy. It should have been a happy day. But then Emilia had said something sharp, and Enri had snapped, blurting out that he knew about her affair.

Which would've meant he learned about me *and her. And Lily.*

My stomach had dropped so fast I thought I might be sick. Because it wasn't just any affair. It was mine.

I'd told myself it was revenge—punishment for the way Enri had handled things when our parents still had custody of Alicia. He'd run off to play happy families with Emilia instead of fighting alongside me. I'd been furious. And when the opportunity came, I'd taken it.

But revenge didn't feel like this. Revenge didn't keep you awake at night, replaying the look on your brother's face. Revenge didn't make you feel like you'd set fire to something you could never rebuild.

Now Enri and Emilia's marriage was a hollow shell, all in name only. And I'd done that.

I shook my head, forcing my eyes back to the screen, but the words blurred. The spreadsheet cells swam. Somewhere in the building, the lift doors opened and closed, the sound echoing down the empty corridor. I told myself I was here to work. But really, I was here because going home meant being alone with the truth.

And the truth was that I was a piece of shit. And I knew it.

I slammed my eyes shut, deciding to call time of death at the late project. Fuck Hanna. She can suck my-

Said appendage rose to attention with little fuss.

I didn't call you, Judas.

I stared at the spreadsheet for another thirty seconds on the laptop before closing it without saving. Hanna could stew over the "incomplete" version tomorrow. If she wanted to play power games, I could play too.

I shut down my computer, grabbed my coat, and slung my bag over my shoulder. The thought of going home to the silence was unbearable, so I decided I'd find somewhere dimly lit, with overpriced cocktails and someone willing to hand over control for the night. A submissive, pliant and eager, would do nicely.

The elevator chimed as I pressed the button, and my mind drifted—unhelpfully—to Emilia.

The last time we'd spoken, she'd been a mess of contradictions. She'd tried to seduce me again, but in the same breath told me she wanted to confess everything to Enri. Said she loved him. Said the thought of him with anyone else made her sick.

It was almost laughable. This was not the Emilia I'd known—the one who could turn cruelty into an art form, who'd once matched me in every calculated move. Now she was soft around the edges, almost… earnest.

I'd tried to stop her, of course. I'd leaned into every trick I knew, every touch and word designed to pull her back into my orbit. But she'd pulled away. And tonight, Enrique would know.

The elevator doors slid open, and I stepped inside, still replaying the conversation in my head. I didn't even notice until I stepped out again that I'd pressed the wrong button.

Enri's floor.

I was about to turn back when I heard it—a faint, irregular sound. Not quite voices, not quite footsteps. Something in me stilled.

I hesitated, then followed the noise down the corridor, my heels clicking softly against the polished floor. The building was supposed to be empty at this hour. The sound came again, sharper this time, from behind a half-closed office door, along with a familiar voice.

I pushed it open.

Well, well, well. Bugger me surprised.

Enrique's average build never stood out. He was always just tall or just short enough for a lot of things. But here, he looked smaller and slight enough for me to almost ignore the fact that he was bent low across one of the desks littered about. A shock of ginger appeared behind his lowered slacks, head bobbing between spread cheeks, as Enri's moans took on a high and frequent pitch. I was horrified, and made to move away but just then, the ginger moved, revealing almond hazel eyes, bright freckles and ruby red lips.

I recognized her instantly as Melody Suran, one of the newer workers, a temp who was slowly making her was up the corporate ladder. She had a good brain on her, and I had nothing unfavorable to say about her. But now-

I know you like eating ass. Specifically, my brother's. When did that happen?

"You sure you're ready to go further? I warned you, this was going to get wild. I need to prepare you."

Enri cut her off.

"I *know* what I'm doing. I'm ready."

"I'm just saying, last time you stopped me, *because* of your wife, now you call be because of her-"

"My *wife* and I are done. She made sure of that. Now I'm getting what I want, just as she did. And what I want," I saw him move as if to strip completely and I closed my eyes, backing away rapidly towards the elevator.

"What I want is that cock so deep inside of my guts that I can taste it."

I nearly tripped over my feet in my black snakeskin pumps.

Did I just hear? Surely not...

I slowly crept back towards the door. I ducked my head in, and my eyes bulged. There wasn't much that surprised me, but the sight of Melody's thick curved cock, rising above Enri's ass menacingly certainly did. It was so hard, it was parallel with her flexing abs, and I could see her drooling vaginal lips just below the base, where balls would typically hang on a male. *Holy fuck. What the shit?!*
My breath left me in a wheeze, and Enri's head darted up. I leapt back and raced for the lift, praying with every inch of my soul that he hadn't seen it was me. I always wore a mild-length mud brown wig over my cropped black hair at work, but my height and build were quite noticeable.

As the door closing chime rang, I almost relaxed. As I opened my eyes, I saw Melody's almond eyes gazing straight into mine as the doors closed.

Oh fuck.

Printed in Dunstable, United Kingdom